WASHINGTON'S
SHADOW

WASHINGTON'S SHADOW

Barbara N. McLennan

Washington's Shadow

Published by Gatekeeper Press
2167 Stringtown Rd, Suite 109
Columbus, OH 43123-2989
www.GatekeeperPress.com

ISBN (paperback): 9781642375640
eISBN: 9781642375657

Printed in the United States of America

CONTENTS

PROLOGUE

BURR POWELL, A plump and balding man of forty-three and member of Virginia's General Assembly, sat in the library of his Middleburg farmhouse at a table covered with documents. His younger brother Cuthbert stood behind him, peering over Burr's shoulder. They looked over a pile of account books and letters. Cuthbert, tall, thin and sporting a full, dark moustache, was the recently elected mayor of Alexandria, Virginia. The two were looking through their deceased father's papers.

Leven Powell had died a month earlier while visiting friends in Pennsylvania. The year was 1810. James Madison was president of the United States and the country, officially neutral in foreign affairs, feared being dragged into a great European war for or against Napoleon.

Burr reached into his pocket and pulled out a letter he'd received from his father ten years earlier. "I thought you'd enjoy reading this. It gives some perspective. Maybe we should write a biography of the colonel."

Cuthbert smiled at his brother. "He loved being addressed as colonel. Though he dearly loved Mother and the family, I think his greatest love was for Washington and the revolution. Who'd you have in mind? Little sister Anne, our best writer, has seven children of her own."

Burr smiled in agreement. "Maybe Jane could do it. She's also our sister and lives with Mother; she's been a school teacher, is a fine writer and has seen most everything with her own eyes. Just read this and see what you think. It will help us organize the rest."

Cuthbert sat down next to Burr, took the yellowing pages from him, and read:

February 12, 1801

Dear Burr,

I know you cannot help but wonder why I write to you at this black hour of the republic. As you know, I am here in the House of Representatives because the General, in the last year of his life, asked me to stand for Congress for our new county of Loudoun. I understand his meaning now, as with Jefferson and Burr tied in electoral votes, the House must now elect the president. But I am only one vote among one hundred forty-six members and this vote is by state.

We are hopelessly tied; twenty-four ballots already and no candidate has won a majority of our sixteen states. Since the revolution, we've added three—Kentucky, Tennessee, and Vermont. It looks like eight states are for Jefferson, but he needs nine to win; the rest are split between Adams, Burr and Pinckney. Vermont is split and doesn't cast a vote at all.

What can I tell you? You know I've always distrusted Jefferson and didn't vote for him the last chance I had, in 1796. He's a scurrilous exaggerator and liar and though he writes about revolution and independence with great enthusiasm, he knows nothing about living in a place torn by war. He's never worn a uniform and loves radical speech. He might as well be French, he loves them so much. He would tear our Constitution to shreds, and that's the only thing that holds us together. He has no living memory of the Articles of Confederation; he'd simply amend them so the President could do as he likes. Without a Congress and without courts, he'd place himself above all of that, like Napoleon.

I've spent my life trying to make a living for my family, much the same as most people. My goodness, I'm no military man but I've served in militias my whole life, as my father did before me. I've been part of a militia since Lord Dunmore's War against the Indians all the way back in 1774. I had a farm and a mill and six children. I left your poor mother to take care of everything and wrote to her almost every day, as I'm writing to you now.

I fear the country is at a crossroads. I've met all the candidates and fear the outcome. You know I've met Mr. Aaron Burr, who surprised everyone when he tied Jefferson in the electoral college. I've found him to be sensible and he is a veteran of the revolution, having fought in Quebec and Monmouth Courthouse. We first met years ago at Valley Forge, where we both suffered greatly. Though I don't subscribe to his party, I support some of Burr's ideas. Many Federalists support him over Jefferson. He would end slavery and grant women the right to vote. That makes him popular in the new states, especially Tennessee. God knows, your mother has more sense than most and it would do no harm to widen the suffrage to all who work for a living as Burr wishes. Jefferson fancies himself an aristocrat and would have none of this.

Hamilton considers Burr to be dangerous and has begged us all to support Jefferson. Hamilton keeps busy writing letters to all of us asking us to switch votes from Burr to Jefferson. I'm undecided. Though the Congress is Federalist, Adams' support is confined to a few northern states and he can't get a majority of all the states.

I want to do what my constituents would want me to do. I won't do anything unless Burr asks that Jefferson be elected President; Burr would then become Vice President. Burr has got to be careful, as he is out of his element here in Washington, and Hamilton is working against his interests in his home state of New York.

Well, I feel better putting this in writing, though I don't know where it leaves the country. I'm afraid we are electing a president with our eyes closed, like pinning the tail on a donkey. The donkey is our country.

Remember me to the family and grandchildren. Your mother keeps well but would rather go back to Middleburg. She doesn't care for our new capital city, with its mud and ruts everywhere. Even the new capitol building is no beauty. It's just a giant square box, and the members feel like small rats roaming its corridors.

Affectionately,
Leven Powell (Colonel)

PART ONE
MIDDLEBURG AND ALEXANDRIA, 1810

CHAPTER 1
THE BOYS TALK TO JANE

BURR AND CUTHBERT Powell had different opinions. Neither was much of a writer, though they'd each done their share of public speaking. Burr, the second son to Leven and closest to their mother, feared that the idea of writing a biography of Leven would upset her. Sally Powell was herself near seventy years of age and had suffered her share of illnesses. Cuthbert thought she'd love the idea, though he wasn't sure how their sister Jane would like the job. Burr wanted a long talk with Jane before anything was decided.

After all, the Powell children numbered eleven and there were more than fifty grandchildren; Cuthbert himself was father to ten. Their mother had told them many times that between running the flour mill, putting food on the table, and making sure everyone could read and write, she could start her own country. She knew exactly who could do what, and she'd done just about everything whenever Leven had been away from home. In the early days of their marriage, that took place frequently.

Burr and Cuthbert arrived at their childhood home in Middleburg early in the afternoon. They tied their carriage to the rail by the side of the large farmhouse and noticed that they weren't the only visitors. Several carriages and horses had already arrived and they could hear children shouting in the rear vegetable garden along with the deep voice of their brother Billy.

"Sister Anne and Billy, together under the same roof?" Burr grimaced, pulling in his large pot belly.

Cuthbert shrugged. "She's brought some of her brood. I guess the idea is to keep Grandma so angry and busy she can't think. I wonder if Jane is hiding somewhere."

When they entered the main room of the house, they could see bags and packages belonging to their sister and brother, along with clothing of every size draped over the chairs and tables of the large room. Over a screen near the fireplace, children's clothes were drying, and various cups and plates were lying in virtually every corner of the room.

From the kitchen they heard their mother calling out, "Is someone else here? Come into the kitchen for some biscuits."

Burr and Cuthbert went into the kitchen and noted that there already were too many people for them to get near the newly baked biscuits. They could see their mother, sister Anne and four of Anne's children. They didn't see Jane.

Burr approached his mother and they embraced. He could see she'd been crying, but with a house full of grandchildren she'd put her sorrow aside. He whispered in her ear, "Cuthbert and I are here. Can we talk later?"

She said nothing. She still wore widow's weeds, a black dress covered by a white apron, and a white cloth cap on her head. She was a small woman but still had good use of her hands. She could bake and cook and keep the place tidy. That was how she dealt with sorrow; she kept doing things. Though she had two servants who assisted her, they sometimes couldn't keep up with everything she wanted done. The servant women, Nancy and Dorothy, were over sixty and themselves were grandmothers many times over. They'd been part of the Powell household for more than forty years, since the first arrival of Powell children.

Cuthbert next came over to his mother's side. He said, "So much to do? It's time you let someone serve you, Mother. How about a walk in the back woods? It's June and the sun shines. I'll take a blanket and we can pick some flowers."

She smiled at the thought, but said, "A lovely idea, but grandmothers know which end is up. Four grandchildren and your brother Billy need to be fed. Why don't you boys take Jane down to the stream? She'd love that."

Burr asked, "Where is Jane? Not outside with Billy and the little boys?"

"Of course not. She's upstairs with her door bolted. Maybe you can talk her out of there."

The two brothers looked at each other and Burr turned to Nancy and Dorothy to ask them to prepare a small picnic basket. "We'll take Jane out for a bit. We'll take the carriage and go a little farther down the stream to where it's quiet."

An hour later, Burr, Cuthbert and Jane sat on a blanket next to a fresh fast-running brook, eating a light picnic lunch. The two men swallowed their beers; Jane picked at some ham and biscuits.

Jane, a woman in her thirties, had an expressive oval face and dark hair showing a few strands of gray. Not exactly beautiful, she was striking. Although she was not very tall, she had a square, powerful body. Dark bushy eyebrows made sharp arches over her deep brown eyes and when she spoke her voice surprised; she was almost a baritone. When Jane Powell spoke, people listened.

A trained school teacher, Jane knew how to frame an argument. She'd been her mother's favorite helper in raising the younger Powell children, and she still cared for her mother. She'd never married.

Burr began. "Jane, how goes it with Mother? Is she keeping well?"

"You should know by now. Whenever she's on her own, she keeps busy, even with silly make-work projects. It's been a blessing to have Anne and the four little ones. Billy's another matter."

"How so?"

"He's in debt and thought with Father gone he'd have some easy inheritance. To his disappointment, Father left everything to Mother."

"He got nothing?"

"Not only that, Father left a note with Mother stating that Billy was not to receive anything unless he could show he'd paid off his debts to two merchants who'd pestered Father. After that he was to receive a small sum, I think fifty dollars. We fear he won't go home now, as he'll pester Mother for the money until she relents. You know he always did that with Father."

Cuthbert smiled and looked at Jane. "How can we help?"

"Oh, Billy is older than you, Burr. He's always been special to her and he takes advantage."

Burr stood up and moved over to Jane and sat on the blanket beside her. Cuthbert stood and leaned against a tree where he could hear his brother speak.

Burr began to state his proposal. "Jane, we have been going over some of Father's papers. We have some of his letters and other documents. Do you think you could look at them?"

"Why?"

"Well, you know, he knew the general. He was at Valley Forge. He was an elector in 1796 and in Congress for the election of 1800. We thought the family should know all of that in a way they could appreciate. You can write a little biography."

"Little? That sounds like a healthy project for big political boys like you two. Why do you ask me when you have the materials? You evidently know what you want it to say."

"Would you say something different?"

"I was with Mother through all of that. I'd have her perspective and mine, not Father's. That might be a biography you won't want to read."

"Why? Mother's met the general. She shared Father's life of building a business and moving west. A biography that includes the women would be wonderful for our girls."

Cuthbert interrupted. "Jane, you're a teacher and you see the different sides of complicated issues. You know how to make an argument. I think Father would want you, more than anyone else, to put his life on paper for the children and grandchildren to see."

"Now I see how you were elected mayor in Alexandria. A silver tongue, but when am I supposed to do this? Now we have Billy. Anne will probably leave with the children in the next week, but then we have a lot of work in the garden. And you saw the house, didn't you?'

Cuthbert smiled. "Yes, I know. As mayor of Alexandria, I can make this promise: I'll take Billy home with me where he will be put to work in a law office, doing very tedious things. He'll be able to work off his debts and get his fifty dollars. If he refuses and says he wants to go west instead, I'll give him two horses and the name of a carriage maker. I'll also send two men to you to help clean up the garden. How does that sound?"

Jane thought. She stood up and walked down to the little creek where she washed her hands and face. When she came back, she said, "Let me see the papers and I'll give you my answer in a week or so. But you have to take Billy."

The two brothers agreed, and the following morning Burr brought over a box containing the Leven Powell papers. Cuthbert left with Billy, who refused to go to Alexandria with him. Instead, he planned a trip to the mountains and Winchester, far away from his creditors. Cuthbert gave him two horses and twenty dollars.

CHAPTER 2

JANE AND MOTHER
HAVE A TALK

JANE OPENED THE box of her father's papers only after her sister Anne, Anne's children, and Billy were safely away and the house tidied. It took two days for the four women to pick up the mess that had been left by visitors and guests over the prior three weeks. Anne had been the fourth of the Powell children to visit Grandmother Powell. Each had brought three or four small children of their own, and all had kept the house on edge with the normal loud games and shouts of small cousins playing with each other. Their grandmother loved each of them, but after three weeks she was tired.

Jane saw to it that her mother rested at least during the heat of the day. Virginia summers were hot and humid, and this year was no different. With her mother resting in an easy chair by the fireplace, Dorothy knitting in a corner chair, and Nancy preparing the evening meal in the large farmhouse kitchen, Jane placed the strange heavy box on a table usually used for holding breads and baked items.

Nancy and Dorothy moved closer to the table to examine the large crate, while Sally stayed in her chair. Constructed of dark leather with black straps and an elaborate clasp to hold the lid down, the box looked out of place in the kitchen.

Sally asked Jane, "Have you found Blackbeard? Is this a treasure chest?"

"A good guess. But no, not Blackbeard's. This contains the papers of Colonel Leven Powell, Esq., friend to all who knew him and receiver of all sorts of letters himself."

Dorothy touched the box lid. Partially descended from Ohio Indians, she was tall and dexterous. She knitted socks, sweaters, and scarves for her own twenty grandchildren as well as selected items for the Powell progeny. The box had caught her eye; she'd never seen that sort of detailed workmanship applied to leather. Dark and light leathers had been sewn together and the top of the box displayed carved images of intertwined flowers and birds. Dorothy's knitting generally kept to traditional Native American red and gray geometric designs and the carved flowers fascinated her.

When Jane opened the box, Dorothy and Nancy inched closer to see how the lid would come open. Sally, still in her chair, remembered this old box, a gift from her father to Leven soon after the opening of the flour mill some fifty years earlier. Her father knew Leven would be a careful bookkeeper and the box was supposed to hold his most treasured papers.

Jane turned to her mother. "Would you like to see what we have here, Mother? There might be some things in your own hand."

Sally looked up, near tears. "Too soon for me to look at those old things. Why are they here?"

"The boys, Burr and Cuthbert, thought it might be a good idea to prepare a little biography of Father. They asked me to do it. What do you think?"

"Father wouldn't have wanted anything like that done for him.

He never wanted his name on anything, if he could avoid it. He certainly wouldn't have wanted a pompous promotion of some hero to be put forward and attributed to him. Just like Burr to think of such a thing!"

"Well, I wouldn't prepare that kind of piece. I knew Father well and can read between his lines about as well as anyone he knew."

Nancy viewed the yellowing papers in the box, covered with the small delicate handwriting of Leven Powell. Of partial African descent, she was a large woman who loved to cook. She also read and wrote whenever she could, thought deeply about what she read, and always shared her thoughts freely. She and Dorothy were free women, married to free men.

Because of his Quaker ancestry, Leven Powell always refused to keep slaves. Sally, his wife, wouldn't have servants who couldn't read, write, and keep accounts, and she'd taught Nancy and Dorothy all she knew. Nancy, of all the women in the room, had the finest handwriting. Nancy remarked. "What a wonderful hand he had. We could read out his letters slowly, a few each night. It would be like having him here again with us. It will bring back memories."

"Leven wouldn't have wanted that. He wasn't for sitting back to remember. He was always pushing ahead," Sally said.

Jane looked at her mother. "Would you rather we not look and not write anything? The boys will be disappointed."

Dorothy, the most religious of the four, chimed in. "He's gone on to the next world, but has left all of this for us, the children, and the grandchildren. But I think Miss Sally is right. We should do it in a way that shows the real Leven."

Jane nodded her head in agreement. "I know. The boys asked me to do it, while Father's longest letters were to them. To us, he only made simple requests or wished us well, without much thought. It was as if he believed that Mother and the family could do well enough without his advice and commentary."

Sally shook her head. "He never understood what it was like without him here. When his letters came, they were read, but not always right away. There was always so much for all of us to do to keep going. Maybe your biography should tell our story as well, though the boys probably won't want to hear that part of it."

"So, you think I, or we, should do this?"

The four women agreed to go through the box together. After a week, Jane had the papers arranged by year and subject. She sent a message to Burr that she would try to write something, putting it all together in one small essay.

CHAPTER 3

BEGINNING

"HOW SHOULD WE start this, Mother?"

Jane thought about how to begin writing about her father. In addition to the documents, Mother was going to be a great resource. Jane wanted her mother to do more than just accept the project; she wanted her to take it on as her own, to share her memory and insight. She wanted her mother to evaluate the documents, not simply read and remember them.

Sally looked up from a vest she was mending. Billy had left it under a pillow and she couldn't help herself; she had to repair a few tears and resew the seams. "Why not start at the beginning? I was born in 1740, the eleventh of twelve children and youngest of five daughters. Leven was born in 1737. He was the oldest of eight."

Jane smiled. "Was he romantic? Did you have a long or short courtship?"

Nancy and Dorothy entered the room and took seats. Dorothy hummed, "Oh, we'll soon be singing songs and writing poetry."

Sally looked at Dorothy. "Only your George could do that. I still remember him singing out loud by the back door, as if you were the only one who could hear him."

That brought a laugh from Nancy. "My Bob knew he had to put everything in writing. I loved poetry, and he did his best at it."

Jane asked, "Do you have the poems?"

"No, darlin'. Bob found them one day and showed them to our Billy. I don't know where they are now. Miss Sally, tell us about Mr. Leven."

"There's nothing to tell. He was in and out of our house all through his youth. My father and his father were colonels together in the Prince William militia. Also, his mother and my mother were second cousins. He never looked at me until our two fathers decided we should be married."

Jane sat up. "Could you have refused?"

The three older women laughed out loud. "Would you refuse two colonels in the militia?"

Jane looked at them. "I refused several, and my father Leven was a colonel in more than just the militia."

Sally looked at her daughter. "You are smarter and sturdier than I was and were looking for something else." Sally took a deep breath. "Is that my fault? Did I spoil you? Should we have demanded that you pick a fellow?"

Jane shrugged and said nothing.

Sally continued, "I wanted to have my own family and so did Leven. We understood what we wanted for our future. The first long conversation we had was about what he would do with my poor dowry. He wanted to go west, buy land, and start his own business. He was excited and exciting. I was done with being the bottom of the barrel and last in line. I said I was for the marriage and the families were pleased to have both of us off their hands. My mother had never paid much attention to me."

Nancy said, "That's the truth. It was a hard life then, and to survive people had to keep moving. I had no dowry, but my folks gave Bob and me a mule and wagon and five dollars. That's how we got here, started a farm, and started our family. Like a lot of folks, we went west aiming for Winchester or the Ohio. We lived off the forest, fishing and hunting for at least two years."

Dorothy joined in the reminiscing. "My family lived a little west of this region for as long as anyone can remember. When George came to our village, he had some pots and cutlery that were hard to come by. He offered them to my father, who ran a trading post. My father gave him an argument over the price. George spotted me and gave me a wink and a ceremonial bow. Then he sang an old song in his high tenor voice. He'd brought a guitar with him. My father sent him away.

"He came back every day for two weeks with the same pots, but a different song. Finally, my father told him that he should keep the pots and take me as a wife. I refused because nobody had asked me, and I had quite a few boys from the village hanging around who might ask me. Our neighbors included a few French, some Piscataway, some Cherokee, and some mixed like my family. I didn't really mean it though; three weeks later George took me and we ended up near here. We built a small house on a tract near the carriage stop, Chinn's Ordinary. George became Chinn's bartender and I cooked three days a week for the inn residents. The ordinary was the only place to stay then. A year later I was helping out here."

Sally, anxious to stand up and start doing things, said, "What good is all this remembering? Does it help you, Jane? How does it connect to Father's papers?"

Jane thought before answering. "I was around for a lot of this and only a child for the early part. It helps to know how adults looked at the real world then. I was going to start with Lord Dunmore's War. What do you think of that?"

All three of the older women thought and whispered. Finally, Sally said, "Lord Dunmore was the last English governor and a fool in many ways. Over the first ten years living in this county we three built families and lives for ourselves, all without the help of the English. When your father came here, he was young, in his twenties, but he'd already been a deputy sheriff. When we came to this land, we bought Chinn's, five hundred acres and an old flour mill. We hoped to start a complete town. Leven was forever writing letters and making visits to the east, trying to get people to come and open shops. We started a town bakery with a large oven to provide bread for people who couldn't necessarily afford it; we saw that nobody in this territory starved. That was the beginning of Middleburg."

Nancy continued, "That's how I met your family. We used the flour mill, which your father named Sally Mill after your mother. I was expecting my first baby at the time."

Sally, saddened, said, "Yes, we'd lost our first two, my little Elizabeth and baby Leven. Leven thought I should not work so hard when carrying a child. You were a godsend, Nancy."

"Yes, I was there for Billy's arrival, and he came out fighting. What a baby!"

Sally said, "Well, since this is for our families, you may as well get it right. Dorothy came to help just after Billy was born. She brought her two with her and stayed a few days a week; Nancy came the other days. When they were having their babies, I went over to their places to help, taking you children with me. No matter where we were, we never had fewer than five youngsters at one time. We finally added a school room to the small church across the street from the bakery and hired a teacher. We gradually added a few shops each year, and it became a real community. When Leven left for Lord Dunmore's War, I had five children and we believed we had a real town here."

CHAPTER 4

THE LOUDOUN
RESOLUTIONS

JANE TOOK HER inkwell and quill pen to a table near a window that looked out into the vegetable garden. Though the day was warm, she faced east, and an oak tree shaded that side of the house. She lifted the quill, saying, "I'll start with 'Lord Dunmore, his war, and the education of Leven Powell.'"

Sally commented, "A little grandiose, don't you think? Leven knew Lord Dunmore, but certainly received no education from him. If you want to be properly historical, shouldn't you start with the Loudoun Resolutions? Burr will remember that. Father made sure his boys knew every word he wrote, though they were quite young at the time. You were only three or four and probably paid little attention."

Jane thought about it and responded, "I think I remember what I was told more than my own memory. I remember Billy telling Burr that the resolutions were important."

Nancy smiled at that. "Yes, Billy was the true revolutionary. He loved every part of making a statement and threatening a fight over it. Of course, he was only nine or ten at the time, and ten- year-olds love a good fight."

Sally retorted, "But not everyone in Loudoun wanted a fight. We had meeting after meeting, never agreeing on anything. Then some people would walk out altogether. I don't remember who supported the idea any more, but Leven was in the forefront for independence. He always thought the only thing to expect from the crown was a tax bill for which we'd receive nothing in return. Back then, they were threatening his way of life. He looked west and wanted new lands opened. We welcomed everyone here; we were a main way-stop to the west."

Dorothy poured tea for the other three, poured herself a cup, and took a deep breath. She had a different perspective. "We came east, not west. George was looking for a town and didn't want to live off the woods. Like my father, he wanted a business where he could meet people. He liked human companionship. A tavern job was perfect for him; he hated a fight. But Lord Dunmore would have stopped traffic to the west altogether and he was out to kill as many Indians as he could."

Jane took her pen and wrote, "In June 1774, Leven Powell attended a meeting of freeholders held at the courthouse in Leesburg and presented his neighbors with the Loudoun Resolutions, a document he'd prepared with the help of some friends." While Jane copied the resolution, she read it aloud, as follows:

"PUBLIC MEETING IN LOUDOUN IN 1774. At a Meeting of the Freeholders and other inhabitants of the County of Loudoun, in the Colony of Virginia, held at the Court-house in Leesburg, the 14th June, 1774-F. PEYTON, Esq., in the Chair-to consider the most effectual method to preserve the rights and liberties of N. America, and relieve our brethren of Boston, suffering under the most oppressive and tyrannical Act of the British Parliament, made in the 14th year of his present Majesty's reign, whereby their Harbor is blocked up, their Commerce totally obstructed, their property rendered useless-

"Resolved, That we will always cheerfully submit to such prerogatives as his Majesty has a right, by law, to exercise, as Sovereign of the British Dominions, and to no others.

"Resolved, That it is beneath the dignity of freemen to submit to any tax not imposed on them in the usual manner, by representatives of their own choosing."

Sally stood at that and went to the hearth where she warmed her hands over the fire. "You've made me feel cold with this. It's a shock to think that we lived through so much since we came up with the resolutions." She stood over a large pot that contained the evening stew.

Nancy stood up to join her and suggested, "I think we could use some more vegetables."

Dorothy was already slicing potatoes and carrots at the other end of the table where Jane sat with her papers. Dorothy reminisced, "Yes, I remember George's remarks about the resolutions. He'd been present in Chinn's when Leven and his friends talked about writing resolutions. The beginning was to be all lawyer talk. They had to say that we loved the king but wouldn't pay his taxes."

Jane continued to read as she wrote:

"Resolved, That the Act of the British Parliament, above mentioned, is utterly repugnant to the fundamental laws of justice, in punishing persons without even the form of a trial; but a despotic exertion of unconstitutional power designedly calculated to enslave a free and loyal people.

"*Resolved*, That enforcing the execution of the said Act of Parliament by a military power must have a necessary tendency to raise a civil war, and that we would, with our lives and fortunes, assist and support our suffering brethren of Boston, and every part of North America that may fall under the immediate hand of oppression, until a redress of all our grievances shall be procured, and our common liberties established on a permanent foundation."

Sally commented, "That was controversial and there were heated arguments over the language. Leven knew war was coming and that our militia wasn't a match for troops the British were already sending over."

Nancy stirred the pot and said, "How about I bake a few cakes for tonight? You know, we're working hard now. This old brain has trouble remembering the exact words we said, but I can picture what Mr. Leven looked like. He was determined. He wasn't looking for war, but he wasn't shrinking from it either. Other folks wanted to just hide from what was going on."

Jane kept writing and reading:

"*Resolved*, That the East India Company, by exporting their tea from England to America, whilst subject to a tax imposed thereon by the British Parliament, have evidently designed to fix on the Americans those chains forged for them by a venal ministry, and have thereby rendered themselves odious and detestable throughout all America. It is, therefore, the unanimous opinion of this meeting not to purchase any tea or other East India commodity whatever, imported after the first of this Month.

"*Resolved*, That we will have no commercial intercourse with Great Britain until the above mentioned Act of Parliament shall be totally repealed, and the right of regulating the internal policy of N. America by a British Parliament shall be absolutely and positively given up."

The three older women laughed out loud. Dorothy finally said, "We here in Loudoun weren't exactly involved in trade. It was easy for George, who was a bartender, to say he wasn't going to buy tea. We had only a few shops."

Sally remarked, "Yes, but it was a way to say we support Boston against the British, and we didn't want the British to mess with us. We said that the whole country from north to south felt the same way. We really didn't know if that was true, but our resolutions said so. We were talking ourselves into revolution."

Nancy continued, "Revolution is an odd word here. You know the resolutions speak of avoiding civil war. They don't demand independence. And the resolutions were aimed at the Parliament and acts of Parliament, not the king. But you can see the heart of Mr. Jefferson's Declaration of Independence here. The resolutions said what was wrong and what we wanted to make right and what we would do about it. Still, refusing to buy tea is different than declaring war. There should have been a way of negotiating out of those problems."

Sally shook her head in disagreement while she sat and helped Dorothy cut vegetables. "I think that's a common way of saying we could have done better, but in retrospect there was no other way. The British had a mighty army and cared nothing for the people who lived here. They thought they didn't have to hear our point of view. We thought this was our country. We lived here. We built the towns, tilled the fields, and looked west. We were telling them that we would fight for our homes and our way of life."

Jane remarked, "I suppose most wars are like that. This was already our own country and had been for a long time. The Powell children and grandchildren have no idea what it was like to be a colony or plantation belonging to someone else. I certainly don't remember feeling I was anything different than a Virginian or American. Let me finish:

"*Resolved*, That Thompson MASON and Francis PEYTON, Esqs., be appointed to represent the County at & general meeting to be held at Williamsburg on the 1st day of August next, to take the sense of this Colony at large on the subject of the preceding resolves, and that they, together with Leven POWELL, William ELLZEY, John THORNTON, George JOHNSTON and Samuel LEVI, or any three of them, be a committee to correspond with the several committees appointed for this purpose."

Jane ended by saying, "The Loudoun Resolutions were signed by fifty-one Loudoun freeholders. Feelings against the crown ran high throughout the county."

Sally shook her head, indicating her memory of the final acceptance of the resolutions. She interjected, "Yes, every county passed some resolution. This was before 1776; we weren't declaring independence. We were stating our dissatisfaction with actions taken by the Parliament and crown. Leven was strong in his criticism of the governor and what he represented. He worried for his family and livelihood. He was for helping people who wanted to move west. Other people here were newcomers; some had come from terrible hardships in Europe and didn't want to look back. They loved the idea of a distant king but would do nothing to oppose his governor's orders."

CHAPTER 5
LORD DUNMORE AND WASHINGTON

DOROTHY REMINISCED. "JUST after we adopted the resolutions, Lord Dunmore came here on the way to his war. They were all here. Nancy and I both cooked and served drink that day."

Nancy sat down next to Dorothy and faced Jane. She said emphatically, "Dunmore was an ass; a red-headed Scotsman with a temper to match. We served him at Chinn's. He knew how to drink, but no food was good enough. He threw things about."

Jane was curious. "How would you describe him?"

"He came to these parts dressed in ceremonial clothes," Nancy continued. "He was the great leader of the Virginia militia, but really a small man with a squeaky voice. He wore a kilt and a ruffled shirt but couldn't speak in a way that anyone could understand. When he gave orders, people would look at each other trying to figure out what he wanted."

Jane asked, "But how could he govern like that? How did he deal with the burgesses and the people when they presented him with issues to resolve?"

Sally, listening carefully, said, "He didn't. He came in 1771 and for more than a year wouldn't let the burgesses meet. He soon started a war with the western Indians. Washington and Jefferson were burgesses, and there already was much anger at the crown. When Dunmore finally convened the House of Burgesses in 1774, he did so to raise taxes to pay for his war. Instead, the House set up a committee of correspondence to send complaints to London. Lord Dunmore had previously been governor of New York. When he got to Virginia, he simply had no ear for other people's opinions."

Dorothy started humming an old tune that soon became an altered version of Yankee Doodle. Then she said, "It was already too late. We knew he couldn't govern us. The crown had issued a rule to stop settlers from moving west into Ohio and Pennsylvania and, wouldn't you know, the settlers were already there. My people had been there, moving back and forth, for who knows how long? Dunmore thought, or hoped, he could simply wave a wand to get his way. After all, he was an English lordship and his daughter was married to one of the king's sons and that without the king's permission!"

That memory brought rounds of laughter from the three older women. They started trading old jokes and ribald comments. Jane finally stopped it; she thought she knew the history. She said, "Let me summarize for you what I know of Lord Dunmore's War. This is my memory, based on what I heard from others. If I'm wrong or incomplete, tell me what's missing." She spoke out loud as she wrote:

"John Murray, 4th Earl of Dunmore, rode into Loudoun accompanied by Colonel Washington and followed by several hundred Virginia militia men. They stopped at Chinn's Ordinary, the main carriage-stop between Alexandria and points west. Lord Dunmore, dressed for war, motioned for Washington to speak to the troops. Leven Powell, colonel in the Loudoun militia, listened near the doorway of Chinn's and noted the appearance of the two leaders of the small army.

"Though both were in military dress and sat upon great stallions, Lord Dunmore's head, on which he wore a Scottish tam with feather, was level with Washington's shoulder. Washington wore no hat and had tied his brown hair behind his neck.

"Leven had heard of Washington, but had never seen him before. Washington still was celebrated throughout Virginia for his bravery and heroics in the 1760s war with the French and Indians in Pennsylvania. To Leven, Washington looked like a hero.

"Washington smiled briefly and called to the men to dismount and camp in a field behind the carriage stop. Leven stepped forward and said, 'Welcome to Loudoun, sirs. I am Leven Powell of the Loudoun militia and invite you to partake of food and drink in and behind the ordinary.'

"Washington and Dunmore entered the small inn and took a table while Leven ordered beer for them. A few barrels of beer were brought out to the rear for the refreshment of the troops.

"Leven observed Dunmore and Washington. They barely spoke to each other and Leven approached the table. 'May I join you? We have some chickens roasting if you'd like something to eat.'

"Washington immediately responded, 'Please sit. Tell us about this place.'

"Leven motioned to Dorothy and Nancy to prepare some food for their guests.

"Leven, thirty-five years old and father of five at the time, wasn't used to sitting down at a table during the day. He normally spent his full day tending to his flour mill and the ordinary. Though his hair was thinning on top, he was stocky and powerful in his arms and shoulders. When he sat he could see that Lord Dunmore was a slightly built man while Washington was enormous.

"'My Lord Governor, Colonel, I came to these parts some ten years ago with a new wife from Prince William. I bought this ordinary, five hundred acres, and built a flour mill. We have nearly a hundred families living here now. I've been acting as representative of the community in seeking families who will come and open shops here. We're proud of our little village.'

"Washington asked, 'Do you have problems with the Indian Nations nearby?'

"'Not really, though we're protected by the mountains in the near west,' Leven replied. 'I believe you will find them as you follow the Potomac up into Maryland and Pennsylvania, about a day's ride from here.'"Nancy served the two guests plates of chicken and biscuits. Lord Dunmore sniffled at the food, and Washington immediately began to eat with relish. 'Eat up, my lord; this is proper country food! Gives us strength to go riding.'

"He turned to Nancy and asked, 'Have you something for our men?'

"Leven responded, 'We have several pigs on a spit in the back. That should do for many of them, though I'm not sure we can handle such a large company.'

"Washington responded, 'No worry. The men have brought some provisions with them. They will certainly enjoy a bit of meat as they get ready for their mission.'

"Dunmore shoved his plate so it fell to the floor. He stood up and announced, 'Enough. I wish to ride and see the place. Do you have a main road?'

"Leven stood as the Governor stood while Nancy hurried to clean up the mess Dunmore had made. Leven replied, 'This inn is a main carriage stop on the way west. We can take care of horses and carriages and provide some space for travelers to rest. We have regular traffic between here and Winchester in the mountains. The road is marked that far.' The small main bar of the ordinary soon filled with military officers seeking food and beer. Lord Dunmore looked at Leven and then imperiously left the inn.

"Washington could see that Leven felt insulted and angry. He said, 'Please sit. Tell me what you know about the Indians. We all know they've treated some settlers in Kentucky territory cruelly. Mr. Daniel Boone's son and friends were slaughtered by Shawnees, Cherokees and Delawares.'

"Powell sat down and shared his knowledge with Washington, saying, 'Well, I understand that there are two confederations fighting each other. The Iroquois, from the north, support the 1768 treaty which gave them lands that had always belonged to the Shawnee in Ohio. The Shawnee supported the French in the old war. The old war seems to be back again, but now there are settlers living south of the Ohio and they've been victims to both confederations of Indians. Because of the peace treaty, the Iroquois feel entitled to the lands of the Shawnee group and have sent in war parties. They kill every man they find.'

"'Yes, I know. I've been chief engineer for construction of frontier forts. I've been to western Pennsylvania and southern Ohio. I've even built some canals for transportation near the Ohio River. This is my first stop in western Virginia and I'm pleased to make your acquaintance. I'm not here as part of the military campaign,' Washington advised.

"Leven was surprised at this. 'Will you not accompany the Governor in his fight?'

"'No, I have other plans. The burgesses in Williamsburg are establishing a Virginia committee of correspondence to let the crown know of our opposition to his taxes and the Townshend Act's tax on tea. What do you think of all of this?'

"'Sir, I've worked to build a family and village and will do all I can to protect them from threats near and far. I helped write the Loudoun Resolutions that support the people of Boston in their suffering from the British Parliament's blockade of their harbor. The crown has done nothing for us. These Virginia militia men commanded by Lord Dunmore will likely see this war the same way as I do: a diversion; a way to distract them from their real complaints against the crown.'

"'And you're with the militia?'

"Yes, sir. I feel it's my duty.'

"'Well, I have some letters to compose to friends in Williamsburg. Can you come to my tent to help me with them? I can use another hand in writing.'

"Leven stood. 'I'd be delighted to help.' He spent the rest of the day penning letters that Washington signed. At the end, Washington said, 'Thank you for all of your assistance. Let me recommend you to Dunmore; he'll need someone to do this kind of work during his mission, and you'll be a member of the militia suitable to the task. I'll recommend that he make you a captain.'

"Leven was delighted and thanked Washington. The next morning, Washington left, and Leven gave him a prized bottle of Madeira for his journey back to Mount Vernon."

Sally said, "Yes, I remember that Lord Dunmore commanded an army of about 1,700 Virginia militia men. Leven became involved in preparing statements and letters by the governor to the Indians."

"How involved was he in the military side of things?" Jane asked Sally. "Did he go out and fight the Indians?"

Sally replied, "He was an educated man and an officer, and he did what he was directed to do, and that was to keep accounts and write correspondence. When he came back, he didn't speak of military actions. He clearly despised Lord Dunmore."

Nancy continued, "Don't make too much of Washington's celebrity; Mr. Leven acted on his own beliefs about what was good for his town and family. But he did see a leader in Washington, and it was clear that so did the men of the Virginia militia. Lord Dunmore thought he could distract the Virginians with an Indian war; instead he made an army out of them. I think he may have known that day that Virginia had a leader in Washington who would soon rival him. Only six months later the war for independence began, with Washington as chief of the revolutionary army."

CHAPTER 6
WHITE EYES

J ANE HELD UP a piece of paper to show the women. "Father's papers held the following letter from Lord Dunmore to Captain White Eyes. Do you remember White Eyes?"

Sally looked at Jane and said, "Of course. Who can forget? White Eyes stayed at Chinn's many times with his friend, George Morgan. A most impressive man."

Jane was wistful, "Yes," she said, "He was the father of George Morgan White Eyes. Young George and I were good friends. He was a little older than Billy. He was kind and I thought him very handsome. We watched our elders closely, along with Billy. In the beginning, White Eyes negotiated with Dunmore. Father got to know him on the campaign. After Dunmore's war, White Eyes favored the colonists."

Dorothy stood and carried a basket of cut vegetables to the hearth. She stirred them into the large stew pot and pushed hot coals away from the flame so the stew would cook at a slow simmer. She then said, "Captain White Eyes was chief of the Lenape, part of the Delawares. He came from western Pennsylvania and moved into Ohio territory. He was held in high regard by people who knew him. Many Lenape were Christian, but under White Eyes they remained part of the Indian community. He married a British girl who'd been captured by the Lenape in a raid when she was five. Lots of songs and ballads were sung in taverns about them."

Jane said, "Let me read this letter to you."

"Brother Captain White Eyes:

"I am glad to hear your good speeches sent to me by Major Connolly and you may be assured that I shall put one end of the Belt you have sent me into the hands of our great King who will be glad to hear from his Brothers the Delawares and will take a strong holt of it. You may rest satisfied that our foolish young men shall never be permitted to have your lands, but on the contrary the great King will protect you and preserve you in the possession of them.

"Our young people in the country have been very foolish and done many imprudent things for which they soon must be sorry and of which I make no doubt they have acquainted you, but I must desire you not to listen to them as they would be willing that you should act equally foolish with them, but rather let what you hear pass in at one Ear and out at the other so that it may make no impression on your heart until you hear from me fully w'ch shall be so soon as I can give him further information who am your friend and Brother.

"Captain White Eyes will please to acquaint the Cornstalk with these my sentiments also as well as the chiefs of the Mingoes and the other Six Nations.

Yr. sincere friend & Elder Brother,
Dunmore"

Sally remarked, "Yes, I remember Leven saying what an ass Dunmore was and how he couldn't abide his two-faced attempts to give land away to the Indians."

Nancy had begun preparations for baking and Jane moved pen and ink off the table to give her more room. Nancy said, "This was 1774. Lord Dunmore's Virginia militia defeated the Shawnee coalition in Ohio Territory at Point Pleasant in October 1774."

Dorothy added, "I remember 1774 well. We had nothing but fist fights over politics at the ordinary. Remember, the First Continental Congress was meeting at the same time in Philadelphia to oppose the crown's tax policies. There were people who loved the congress and others who hated it to the point they'd come to blows. Washington served as delegate from Virginia and the congress issued a Declaration and Resolves in support of Boston. These were like the Loudoun Resolutions and followed similar reasoning. That didn't stop the fights."

Sally then said, "Oh, but remember how quickly everything changed? The following March Patrick Henry gave his 'Give me liberty or give me death' speech and Virginia was in a war for independence. A month later, in April, minutemen in Massachusetts fought the battles of Lexington and Concord, and in May, the congress appointed Washington Commander in Chief of the Continental Army. Leven joined the Loudoun County Minutemen and became a major in the Continental Army. No more fights at the ordinary; everyone who stayed here was for Washington. Plenty of Tories disappeared."

Jane walked over to the hearth and stirred the stew as Sally added, "You saw George Morgan White Eyes some years later, didn't you? I seem to recall that he went to college later, and you met him in Alexandria."

Jane took a deep breath as memories of an earlier friendship came back. "I thought George had died some years ago, though I don't really know. He used to write me notes and I haven't received any for years. I believe that Chief White Eyes and his wife were assassinated by an American soldier, even though he'd kept his tribe in support of the revolution; isn't that so?"

Dorothy stood up, went to the hearth, and put her arm around Jane's shoulder. Jane looked at her when she said, "Yes, White Eyes was always for Washington. Poor George, but he was lucky to avoid the killers who got his parents. I guess that's a price of war, but it never made any sense to me. The war was over when White Eyes was killed, and by an American. George was close to Billy, as I remember."

Jane stirred the pot and continued, "The Continental Congress knew White Eyes as an ally. When George's parents were murdered, the Congress agreed to send George to the College of New Jersey for an education. The last time I saw him was before he left Virginia for New Jersey. That was in Alexandria. I stayed with Cuthbert at the time. Cuthbert already lived in Alexandria." Jane was choking and near weeping.

Dorothy could see that Jane had lost her train of thought, and tried to change the subject. She said, "Lord Dunmore killed many Indians of all tribes he met. He thought that would make him a hero like Washington, but everyone saw through him. It was too late, but he loved spilling blood, especially Shawnee blood. Some said he wanted to take part of Pennsylvania for Virginia, as if the land were up for grabs. All for nothing; he was a violent ass."

Dorothy and Jane came back to the table and sat. Jane asked, "Why did Father feel the way he did? Was it Washington who convinced him?"

Sally quickly responded, "No. You must remember he was for going west and settling new country. We'd spent our lives doing that and had talked a lot of relatives and friends into doing the same. We were one of the first families in Loudoun, which used to belong to Lord Fairfax. The crown would have put a stop to growth.

The English treaty would have reserved all of the western lands for the native tribes."

Nancy concurred, adding, "That's right. Washington was a hero, but not everyone was ready to abandon home and go marching behind him. Mr. Leven was steadfast from the beginning. I think his talk with Washington steeled him; he was ardent." She smiled, "So was Billy. So was White Eyes."

Jane, still near choking, said, "I wonder what happened to George. He and Billy were good friends and had planned their futures together. My life might have been different, if George hadn't been sent away."

Sally sat down next to Jane and put her hand on Jane's hand. "We can't change the past. No point looking back on regrets." Dorothy and Nancy nodded agreement.

Dorothy decided to stick to the subject. She said, "Remember, the tribes were constantly moving into each other's territory. The Iroquois kept up a constant state of warfare. When they defeated a tribe, they murdered all the men and took the women and children as slaves. White Eyes married one of the captured slaves. Mr. Leven couldn't abide giving up good country to people like that."

Jane had put her pen away. "That's true," she said, "but Father considered White Eyes a friend and a great man."

CHAPTER 7
NEWS ABOUT BILLY

THE FOLLOWING WEEK, a large coach with magnificent carved wood panels and velvet bunting on the windows arrived at the Powell residence. A surprise to Sally, it carried old friends of Leven, George and Mary Johnston. George had known Leven from his first days in Loudoun and was part of the group who'd put together the Loudoun Resolutions. He and Mary were now in their late sixties and living with one of their well-married daughters in Fairfax. The Johnston's son-in-law was a planter, a lawyer active in local politics, and a sometime gambler.

When they arrived, Sally rushed to greet and embrace them. Together they'd been through early poverty, the revolution, and the strangeness of successful grown children. They shared many memories. The Johnstons brought gifts of food and some unidentifiable packages.

When they finally were settled and sitting comfortably near the kitchen fire, Sally gushed, "How wonderful to see you! We've been reminiscing about Leven and it saddens me to know that I've seen all that I'm likely to see."

Mary responded, "But we have family and food on the table. I'm ready for whenever the great Creator decides to take me."

"Have you gone religious?"

"No more than did Washington. I attend church when my daughter insists so she can make a show. Mostly I write long letters to three of my sisters, all younger than I am. What of you?"

"We've had guests and grandchildren for weeks. Now they're gone so I can finally think. Jane has started writing a little essay about Leven, but we haven't gotten too far with that. Likely someone will pop up to visit soon. I've had little time for deep thoughts."

George took a deep breath. "Maybe you will now. We have some unpleasant news. Have you seen much of Billy?" George, short and stout and with a short, clipped grey beard, was a powerful speaker.

Sally looked at George and Mary. "He was here a few days, but then took off again. He had creditors who bothered Leven a bit, but I haven't heard anything from them. I don't know where Billy is now."

George looked serious. "You know, we've always loved Billy as if he were our own. Such a lively boy! He was passionate about everything he did. Always an idealist."

Sally nodded but said nothing and George continued. "One of his so-called creditors, Jack Walsh, claims that Billy stole from him; that he made off with the small treasury of a new building project in Leesburg. He's out to get Billy and is putting together a group of killers to find him. He's angry. Billy should be warned, wherever he is. Walsh is a determined sort and won't give up easily. If Billy didn't do it, it won't matter to Walsh. He'll want Billy's head if he can get it. I think some politics is involved."

"Oh dear. I think he went west and was fully armed, but I don't think we'll see him again soon. I don't know how to contact him. Who is this Jack Walsh? Why do you call him a so-called creditor? What kind of politics? Billy's not a politician and never was."

George thought a while and said, "Well, if our government provided law and order, the likes of Jack Walsh would be in jail.

My son-in-law, John, met him in a card game and learned of the Leesburg scheme. Billy was there at the time. Walsh somehow came into some money and Billy thought he was a partner, together with John. I don't know the details, but the money disappeared the same time as Billy. John has told us nothing in detail, but we know that Walsh is a violent fellow."

Jane had listened carefully. "Wasn't Jack Walsh one of Jefferson's thugs sent out to chase Vice President Burr?"

George looked at the ceiling and said, "Yes. He's been a thug for hire for years. Burr went west after he left the vice presidency. He had a few dozen people with him and George Morgan White Eyes was one of them. They'd met in New Jersey; both were graduates of the College of New Jersey. Billy was a good friend of George Morgan White Eyes, wasn't he?" George tried to seem confident and put a broad smile on his face.

He continued, "Walsh was well paid for trying to chase down Burr, even though Walsh's people finally failed. General Wilkinson bankrolled them, but some people said the money came straight from Jefferson and the White House. Walsh chased Burr across Indian territory. Three years ago, Burr turned himself in to federal authorities in Mississippi Territory rather than risk being shot by Walsh and his men. Burr really isn't a violent man, though of course he managed to kill Hamilton in a duel. I've heard some stories about that, too. Anyway, Burr spent a pleasant few months at Fort Stoddert technically as a prisoner, mostly playing chess with Mrs. Gaines, the wife of the fort's commandant.

"You know, some people claimed that Burr wanted to make himself Emperor of Mexico. With an army of two dozen men? There never was any evidence against him, in Mississippi Territory or later in Virginia. He had a decent trial, presided over by Chief Justice Marshall who was riding circuit. Burr was fairly acquitted, but felt he had to get away from enemies and now is in Europe."

Jane asked, "What happened to Burr's men? Did you hear anything about George Morgan White Eyes?"

George looked at Jane. "Ah, yes, a good friend to you and Billy. George Morgan White Eyes had important relatives, chiefs in Indian territory, and likely was helpful to Burr in setting his travel plans. No, I don't know much else, though I think Walsh knows a bit, and he's after Billy over something connected to Burr's adventures. I think the Leesburg project is just Walsh's excuse so he can round up his gang. Walsh is clever and has spent a lifetime working for devious people."

Mary looked at George, saying, "No need to worry. Billy is a lucky boy; I'm sure you'll see him again and in one piece. But if you know someone who's going out west, you can ask to deliver a message to Billy at one of the trading posts."

Jane said, "Mother, I'll write out something and we'll figure a way to get it delivered."

Sally nodded her head in agreement and said, "So strange. We were just talking about White Eyes. That family suffered much at the hands of hired thugs."

The Johnstons stayed for three days and left gifts for all the Powells, with special packages for Burr, Cuthbert and their families. Before they left, they read Jane's essay, made a few comments, and reminisced about Washington and the old days before the revolution.

CHAPTER 8

BURR REMEMBERS

TWO DAYS LATER, Burr arrived, accompanied by two of his children, John and Beth. They'd ridden horseback all the way from Leesburg and were hungry when they arrived. Nancy accommodated them with sliced ham and vegetables from the garden.

As soon as Burr and the children sat down at the kitchen table, Jane showed Burr the note she'd written. He read it carefully, while Sally asked her grandchildren, "We love seeing you two, but do you have a special reason for coming?"

Burr responded, "I want them to hear what Jane writes about their grandfather. I thought it would bring the revolution alive to them."

Nancy asked, "What would you like to know about Grandfather?"

John, a tall, dark-haired boy of sixteen with very broad shoulders, answered, "We want to know about Washington mainly, and maybe about the war and fights."

Beth, fourteen years old, with blond curly hair which she tied back with ribbons, nodded her head in agreement, but added, "I miss Grandfather. He had such a deep love of country. I thought I could help Jane, if she wanted that."

Dorothy laughed and returned to her knitting. Burr read what Jane had written about Leven out loud while John and Beth listened. Burr read the essay slowly and Jane finally asked, "What do you think?"

Burr tried to remember the events in the essay. "I think I was about John's age when all this happened. My impression of Dunmore was different than you say. His uniform was bright red, and he seemed fierce, even angry. I thought he looked like a man on a military mission. Washington was already my hero and he didn't disappoint. It was as if he were a different sort of being, someone magical. There were stories about him leading battles in the war against the French and Indians and never being shot. Seeing Washington's size, those stories were hard to believe, but people who remembered swore by them."

"Should we continue this way? It's only what we saw and what the papers say. I don't know what Father had to do with Dunmore's letter to White Eyes, but the document was in his papers."

"He probably transcribed it for Dunmore," said Burr. "Likely he kept it because it showed the contempt Dunmore held toward average Virginians. Father knew what he was doing when he supported Washington and independence. Also, Father was a great admirer of White Eyes."

Sally looked at her two grandchildren. "What do you think? If there were no revolution we'd be part of a great empire, instead of a small country on the edge of a wilderness."

Beth responded without hesitation, "Better to be free than slaves to anyone! We'd be for Washington." John said nothing, but didn't disagree.

Sally smiled and asked Burr, "How is Billy faring? Do you know anything?"

"Cuthbert tells me he left him at a trading stop on the road to Winchester. Cuthbert knew the trader and Billy was equipped with a small wagon of blankets, pistols and muskets and a few other items. Billy was determined to drop off the earth. He aimed to go into Indian territory, whatever the dangers."

"I gave Cuthbert a package for him."

"I know. Cuthbert told me he put both books—the Bible and Father's copy of Milton—under the blankets. Billy knew they were there and told Cuthbert that he expected to have time to look at them."

"Well, it will take more than a Bible to protect him where he's going." When Sally said that, Jane asked Burr about the note she'd written to Billy.

Burr took his mother's hand. "I know about all this. I'm taking John out to Winchester to see if we can learn some more about where he is. I know some traders there. We'll do some hunting and trapping. Would you like some furs for the winter?"

Beth looked at her Aunt Jane and quietly asked, "Can we talk?" With that, Jane and Beth stood up and went outside to pick some vegetables.

After they filled two baskets with green beans, Beth finally burst out, "Oh, Aunt Jane, I'd love to help with the writing, but I want to go with them. I can track and shoot as well as John, and Billy's my favorite uncle. Mother didn't want me coming here at all. She thinks I should just dress for parties and get ready for marrying. I let her know that I can visit my grandmother and aunt, same as John. Father relented and said I could help you and that's why I'm here. John had to be dragged into coming as he doesn't like the woods at all."

Jane looked at her pretty young niece and smiled. "Now, let's not get too excited. When I was your age, I was closer to my brothers than anyone. I fished and hunted with them and they were pleased I came along. Let's go in and see what the plans are."

They returned to the house and put the baskets of green beans on the table. Nancy brought over a basket of cut carrots and soon sliced the beans to mix them with the carrots.

Dorothy had put away her knitting and said to Burr, "Go see my cousins and mention me to them. They own the Black Eagle Tavern on the main road. They will tell you what you need to know. And see if you can bring back some woven things. Blankets would be nice."

Jane said, "Yes, we should find out as much as possible. Maybe Walsh has been spotted somewhere or someone who knows him has said something."

"Can I go on to the Black Eagle with you?" Beth asked.

Dorothy looked at Beth knowingly. She said, "Go to Logan's farm and cut through the woods from there. Beth can stay with Amy and Hannah and you can decide what to do after you talk to them."

Jane added, "A good idea. I'll be going to Cuthbert in Alexandria for a few days, delivering some packages for him. Beth wouldn't be much help with the essay until I get back."

Sally said, "Yes, send the Logans our best. We'll have some pies and hams for you to take to them and bring yourselves back as soon as you can."

That evening, Jane, the other women, and Burr and his family talked about the beginning of the revolution in Loudoun. The grandchildren listened for a while, but soon lost interest. Beth felt excited about going out to Indian territory and finding Uncle Billy while John was anxious and nervous about the idea.

CHAPTER 9
THE REVOLUTION BEGINS

A FTER BURR, JOHN and Beth left, the women didn't talk about it, but they all were anxious. Jane went through the box of papers and kept writing.

"Leven returned from Lord Dunmore's War to learn that the Continental Congress had issued its declaration and resolves. Leven, not a military man, took measures to protect his family and the families near him. He purchased guns and muskets for himself and his neighbors. He tried to strengthen the perimeter around the flour mill and he ordered hats and clothing that would serve him if he found himself in colder, more northern climates.

"He talked to his wife and children about the dire times ahead. He knew he'd have to be leaving them on their own when he served in the army.

"Sally knew that Leven had never lived out of doors, nor had he slept in tents, and that he was prone to illness. She worried he'd not be able to keep up with the younger, healthier troops he'd be commanding."

Sally remembered the early days of the war. "Yes, he was anxious for us, but that soon gave way to excitement. You know, in the beginning no one really thought about what a war would really be like. We were way out in the hinterland and almost all families had land to protect and were used to protecting it against varmints large and small."

Nancy remembered, "Everyone who went with the army needed to be equipped, but we didn't know with what. Also, we had to make sure the people left behind knew how to shoot a rifle and herd the cows. That meant the children had to be brought into the idea of a revolution."

"For us, since George took care of the bar and that meant keeping peace in the ordinary," Dorothy continued, "all my boys could shoot from the time they were eight or nine. George always made sure they knew what they were doing, and everyone who came to the ordinary knew what the children were about. It wasn't just using firearms; it was wrestling and all kinds of hand-to-hand combat. I think my girls were the same. Alice was our best shot from the age of seven."

Sally interrupted: "Speaking of best shots, how are we going to know about what's up with Billy?"

"I'll send our Bobby out to the Black Eagle," Dorothy replied, "and let the cousins know there could be trouble. Bobby's a good horseman and will be back in a few days; we'll know what's up from him."

Nancy said, "He shouldn't go alone. Our Daniel is fine on horseback and a good shot. He and Bobby get along well for fourteen-year-olds."

Sally couldn't stand the anxiety. "Couldn't George or Bob go with them?"

Nancy looked at Sally and said, "You're forgetting our age, Ms. Powell. My Bob could never handle riding horseback now, and George is much the same. The older children have farms and businesses and can't get away because they're supporting their families. The youngsters know what they're doing and they're going to relatives who'll look out for them. They'll be happy to be away from chores, and they'll have stories to bring back."

"How do you know how good at shooting they are?" asked Sally. "Everyone tells stories to grandmothers. How do you know what to believe?"

Dorothy looked outside and noticed it was raining, a heavy downpour in July. "Well, I think heaven is listening to us old ladies and weeping. The youngsters should go; this is their country and they should see what they've got and learn to do the right things when it counts. Finding and helping Billy is only part of it. They should see the mountains and the forests and meet the people who are living there; they should see how hard it is to build a community and what it takes to keep it together. If they're not ready for it, we've been bad parents and bad grandparents."

Sally looked at her two servants, more like sisters to her than her own sisters. They'd been through much together. She said, "I think both boys should go. It's safer with two going together."

Jane asked, "Did Father think of what was safe in the beginning?'

Sally answered, "No, it was like a game in the beginning. Leven's first job was to lead his Loudoun militia to harass Lord Dunmore. They all really relished that. Do you remember? That was the first Christmas he spent away from home. We had letters from him."

Jane discovered the letters in the box. The first one read:

"Hempfield Camp, Dec. 3, 1775

My dear—I have been here since Monday, cooped up in a little Dent, exceeding hearty, and pass the time off very agreeably. This morning I have received an Express from below to proceed with my little army, now increased to five companies, to Dumfries, from whence we expect to march to Williamsburg to stop Dunmore in his first career, who has proclaimed Freedom to the slaves, and invited them to the King's standard and take up arms against the country. He has largely increased his army by them and Tories.

I do not know whether it will be in my power to come home before I go down, no other field officer being in camp, every minute of my time is employed. I hope to hear from you by every opportunity and that you want nothing my Estate is able to provide. I have ordered a waggon to call at the Mill for flour; by this waggon please to send my black breeches, and if any safe hand offers, my new little gun also. I am in great haste.

> Your loving husband,
> Leven Powell

"Yes, his little gun!" laughed Sally. "It took me three days to find it; he had it wrapped up in cloth under the bed. Not much use to me there. I had my own pistol handy."

Nancy and Dorothy smiled at first, but soon memories of terrible times took over. Nancy said, "Do you remember Dunmore and his slave army? He had those poor souls herded into a stockade outside Williamsburg. There were no inoculations then and smallpox spread like wildfire. Hardly any survived the first weeks of the war."

Sally said, "Yes. Smallpox took many in the old days. Washington himself was a survivor and his face showed the scars of it."

Jane shifted a few papers and came up with another letter. "This one's dated December 10, 1775. He was very specific in his war news. He wrote:

" . . . The Battle our Boys had with Dunmore's forces . . . turned out more fatal to Dunmore than I knew. It seems that his loss was a hundred and two, and those of his best troops. Out of his favorite company of Grenadiers he has but eleven left and they without officers. Upon his defeat, he has thought it prudent to take to his vessels, and left his faithful auxiliaries—the negroes—to shift for themselves.

" . . . Some few of our men have deserted since we left town; the horrors of war are too much for their puny stomachs."

Dorothy said, "I remember that letter. By the time we received it, Dunmore had entered Williamsburg and emptied the guns and ammunition from the armory. He intended to load his two ships and make off with the arms before the Virginians could seize the stuff. Patrick Henry's militia stopped him. We kept the armaments but let Dunmore himself get away. What a governor!"

"Who were the Loudoun deserters?" Jane asked.

"We had a few Tories and a few cowards. Every town had them," Nancy responded. "There were also people who couldn't stand fighting and killing at close quarters. Nothing happened to deserters then as the army was so new. Now that the war is over, you can't find anyone who wasn't brave or not for Washington in the beginning."

Jane continued reading:

"I received your present of the Venison Ham, which was very acceptable. I've sent the Saddle-Bags in which I return some books which I took with me when I first set out. I sha'nt have time to read them, and they may be lost. The key of the Saddle-Bags I've enclosed. Remember me to the children, my brother and Miss Nancy. . . ."

"He took books to the war?" Jane couldn't believe it.

"He loved his books. You remember how much he read," Sally said. "He valued books dearly. Our neighbor Peter took things back and forth for us, and we made sure for the first few months that he had food to eat."

Nancy said, "It was all so easy in the beginning, as if chasing Dunmore out of Virginia was going to be the whole war. Mr. Leven made sure we got all the details. He wrote long letters from Norfolk and Hampton, described the deaths of women and children in the streets because of British naval ship bombardments from Norfolk harbor. Our side beat Dunmore's troops there, then evacuated and burned what was left of Norfolk so the British wouldn't have port facilities."

Jane held up several other letters. "It may have gotten hot and difficult, but Father writes of cordial meetings with Dunmore and his commanders in Norfolk."

"Yes, I remember," Sally said. "He took much time in writing very detailed letters. Once the battle was over, some loyalist officers and families were left and he met with them. I suppose he didn't have much else to do. Read me from some of them. I seem to remember he had shipboard dinners and attended fancy dress balls. He always complained in his letters that he wasn't feeling well after a night of too much drink. But he once sent a box of oranges that had come up from the Indies."

Jane asked, "What did he expect you to do about him not feeling well?" Nancy and Dorothy, on hearing that, looked at each other and laughed out loud.

Jane continued, "Let me read to you from some of these." Jane read:

"Hampton, January 13, 1776, I arrived here in very good health . . . in which I have remained ever since, except one day . . . owing to intemperance, having dined with a gentleman . . . who makes it a rule to let no one go from his door sober . . . I was a good deal unwell all the next day . . . but cured at night when I met a party of men who were attacked by the enemy . . .

" . . . I called at a man's house who I believe is one of those who can suit himself to any times, and is consequently either Whig or Tory according to the company he is in. I was informed by him of the loss the Enemy sustained when they landed to burn Norfolk, which was 40 negroes and 6 whites . . . our loss only one who died of wounds, except some women and children killed in the streets . . . "

Sally took a deep breath and stopped her sewing. Nancy and Dorothy, who'd been standing near the kitchen fireplace adding vegetables to the pot for the evening meal, shook their heads at the harsh memories. They came over to the table and sat down next to Sally.

Jane continued:

"January 23d . . . Just now returned from a ball and an assembly of fine ladies . . .

"February 24 . . . I have been uneasy at not hearing from you for some time . . . Since my last letter, this neighborhood has been honored by the company of great men . . . [I was] at the head of a flag of truce . . . I had the honor of breakfasting on the best Hyson Tea with the Commodore, General Clinton, Lord Dunmore and several gentlemen Officers. I was received and treated with great politeness by the whole . . . On board the 'Kitty' vessel I found 12 or 15 Officers, the most hospitable, kind people I ever met. Their treatment of me was so exceedingly kind that on my return I sent them a present of 20 bushels of oysters, 30 loaves of bread, a goose and a turkey. It grieves me to see men of such sentiments as those engaged in such a cause."

Jane wanted clarification. "These were British officers?"

Sally said, "Yes, but they were officers on the ships; they weren't connected to the governor. They'd been sent by the British navy to help Dunmore burn Norfolk. When Dunmore's troops landed to burn the town, our men beat them in a fair fight. Of course, Dunmore saw to it that mostly Negroes in his slave army were killed. The truce was to negotiate Dunmore's escape by sea. Leven genuinely liked the naval officers he met. Remember, Leven represented the victor in that skirmish; the losers had to be polite."

Nancy added, "Things changed pretty quickly. After getting rid of Dunmore, Leven and his troops were sent to White Marsh, following Washington into Pennsylvania."

CHAPTER 10
VALLEY FORGE

JANE TRIED TO distract her mother from anxiety over Billy and the grandchildren. She continued with the manuscript and selected a few long letters from Leven that she thought they'd remember. She asked Sally, "How well do you remember Valley Forge? I know we returned here before the snows came, but I remember the cold."

Sally responded, "Who could forget that cold? Our poor men! What a sight they were! No coats, no food, many with no shoes. I was part of a sewing circle organized by Lady Washington. We sewed shirts and knit scarves and socks."

Jane looked at her mother while Nancy and Dorothy entered the kitchen. Dorothy interrupted, advising, "The troops are off. Bobby, Daniel, Susan, her dog Prince and King George, the mule, left yesterday morning and, according to Dave Logan, Henry's brother, they arrived at Logan's farm yesterday. Dave rode over yesterday afternoon, bringing us some of Martha's sewing." Dorothy held up two shawls and a cloth hat for the ladies to see.

Jane brought some cups to the kitchen table and poured tea for the four of them. She said, "That's good to know. We were just talking about Lady Washington's sewing circle at Valley Forge."

Sally and Nancy tried the shawls, one in a pink geometric pattern, the other striped light blue and white. Nancy recalled, "Yes, all the ladies participated in that. But we had so little to work with. I think Lady Washington kept us and the children together so we'd stay out of the wind and sleet." Nancy turned the striped shawl over and said, "Miss Martha does beautiful work with her sewing. Lady Washington would be impressed."

Jane asked, "Why did Washington pick Valley Forge? Why did the soldiers stay with him when the weather got so bad?"

Sally thought about it, and said, "It was perfectly awful, and many young men died of the cold, starvation and disease. They had no coats and no uniforms were provided. We'd lost Philadelphia and the British army lived comfortably and ate well in the city. But Washington was stubborn and a real leader. If he decided something, the troops followed. It was like a test; if Washington could come out of the trial with an army that could work together, we'd have a real country. The men who stayed had to put country ahead of comfort, but they were poorly trained and couldn't do much for themselves. Many couldn't tolerate the hardship and simply went home."

Nancy said, "What could they do? The so-called Continental Congress couldn't deliver anything as there was no money anywhere. Also, thieves and worse took our supplies. Meat delivered came rotten. Mr. Leven sent us home just after the German baron, Von Steuben, showed up."

Dorothy smiled and reminisced. "Oh, I enjoyed the baron. He was perfect for the job. He got the men to march, to keep themselves and their tents clean. I can hear him now, barking out orders in that funny accent. The men admired him. They became a team that worked together with him showing them the way."

Jane held up a letter from Leven, saying, "The place was too cold and what about disease?" She read:

"Near Valley Forge Camp, January 21, 1778.

My dear, Since I wrote you . . . I have had the misfortune to have a severe spell of sickness . . . I was taken with a flux, which, however, left me in 8 or 9 days, and in its place came on the Yellow Jaundice. . . . During the time of the Jaundice I was seized with a small pain in the upper part of the forehead, just over my left eye. This after several days became very troublesome, and at length began to swell, particularly about the eye, and to break out in little sores. The swelling increased until I lost the sight of that eye . . . The Doctor calls it St. Anthony's fire . . . as soon as I am able to travel with safety I think to set out for Virginia. It will be some time before it will be safe trusting my eye in the cold . . . "

Sally remembered, "Yes, he looked awful when he returned about a month after he wrote that letter. He went to bed for a while but was soon up and about the mill. He had a little difficulty reading as the illness affected both of his eyes. But he remained enthusiastic for the revolution. He wrote letters to Washington every week, and eventually Washington appointed him as a fiscal agent for the army. His responsibility included finding suppliers and arranging deliveries of food and uniforms. Leven's suppliers had to be for Washington and for revolution. They had to be willing to wait to get paid but even so, Leven had no trouble finding the right people. Even though suppliers were much more likely to get paid if they worked for the British, the people we knew refused to work with them. Washington trusted Leven for this responsibility. He knew that Leven, having been at Valley Forge, understood how badly the army needed to be armed and fed."

Nancy added, "Yes, I think Valley Forge became a very important place in everybody's idea of the revolution. Even now, so many years later, people who served ask each other where they were in 1778. That's one of the reasons Mr. Leven respected Aaron Burr and distrusted Jefferson. We'd all met Burr at Valley Forge and knew he went on to fight at Monmouth Courthouse, while Jefferson spent the whole war living comfortably among the aristocrats in France."

Sally responded, "Yes, Leven was no philosopher. He understood the political arguments about the rights of man and such, but he was much more impressed by people who showed they were willing to stand up and fight for their principles. He thought Jefferson became tongue-tied by his own philosophy. Jefferson wrote about the rights of man, but when asked if that included women, Jefferson backed off. The same with the slave issue. Jefferson created flowery rhetoric, but never freed a slave."

"Let's be fair," Dorothy mused. "We really didn't ask philosophical questions, did we? Mr. Leven wasn't so much concerned about the rights of man as his own rights. To him, that included the right to move west and he knew that Washington favored western settlement. He never questioned Washington and neither did we. Where Washington led, we followed. Washington started as a hero after an old battle in the French and Indian War. At Valley Forge, he became a national leader, someone magical. I think a lot of us thought of him as a new kind of king, even though he never wanted that."

Sally responded, "Well, remember there were some other generals who thought they could do the military job better than Washington. Somehow that didn't matter. He had developed a mystical kind of support from the troops and they never seriously questioned his leadership. The soldiers who stayed at Valley Forge remained because of Washington. He'd become special, a symbol of the new country. People trusted him even if he made mistakes. People thought he had great strength of character and that he would try to keep his word. That made him different from all those colonial governors we'd had before him."

Dorothy hummed an old hymn and tried the cloth hat, a white piece embroidered in red that sat on the top of her head with a tie around the chin. Nancy put down the shawl and stood up to get some baking ready. Sally folded the shawls and soon stood up to see to the gardening outside.

CHAPTER 11

LEVEN AND JEFFERSON

AFTER THE MORNING chores were finished and the evening meal was safely simmering in the large pot hanging in the kitchen hearth, Jane sat at the kitchen table and thumbed through the large pile of Leven's letters and documents. With Sally, Nancy, and Dorothy still preoccupied with anxieties about Billy, Burr, and now the grandchildren, Jane decided not to burden them with tedious reading. Instead, she posed a question to the three older women, who were now sitting quietly. Dorothy was knitting and Nancy was sewing a new yellow patterned baby dress for her one-year-old granddaughter. Sally mended the hem of an old dress.

Jane asked, "What made Father go into politics? He felt fierce loyalties to Washington and his family and he wanted to make something of the place he lived, but he wasn't a philosopher, was he? He wasn't the kind of person who enjoyed asking for his neighbors' votes. Did he ever really want or even enjoy elective office?"

Sally looked at Jane affectionately and said, "No, Leven never thought of himself as a politician. He was strong in his beliefs, as were his closest friends. After all, they'd been through a war and suffered much together. He became an elector in 1796 because Washington had asked him. The year before, Washington rode out here himself, on his great horse, and stayed with us for a week. You should remember that. Washington was president. The war was over, and we had a Constitution. But Washington decided that 1796 would be his last year as president. He was ready to go back to his plantation and he worried about what would happen to the country after he retired."

The three older women sat down near Jane at the kitchen table and looked at each other. Sally said, "I think we all remember Washington from that week. He was older than when we first saw him, but he still stood very tall. He had a magical presence."

Nancy said, "Yes, we remember him as if he were magic, but we know he really wasn't. He ate and drank and worried just like the rest of us. He needed to know he had supporters. The rough and tumble of elective politics and the criticisms of him by a wild press took a lot out of him."

Dorothy added, "He enjoyed the place out here and its quiet. He loved the land and shared his thoughts with your father. It was as if he needed to unburden himself to someone he knew and trusted. By 1795, Mr. Leven had known Washington for almost twenty years. He'd followed and supported and worked for Washington almost all that time."

Jane asked, "Did Father have doubts about becoming an elector? This was, after all, the first competitive election for president."

That brought laughs and guffaws from all three older women. Sally finally said, "In 1795, here in Middleburg, a place that supported the revolution and Washington's leadership from the beginning, when President Washington comes here to ask you to do something, you don't question his meaning. You simply agree. That's what Leven did."

"Was he happy about it? Did he have doubts? Wasn't Burr already in the General Assembly?" Jane persisted. "I seem to remember that Father didn't exactly support Burr's choice of a political career."

Sally smiled at Jane and said, "You know Burr as well as anyone. You know he always wanted to feel important and to have a title like Member of the Assembly. Burr was a politician from the time he was a little boy. He knew how to wheedle and complain and was very persistent. Leven accepted Burr's choice to run for office, but never really understood why he needed that."

Jane replied, "Yes, we have long letters between Burr and Father discussing the electoral college. I guess with Burr in the General Assembly, Father thought he knew something about the system."

Sally replied, "I remember him writing those letters. The choice was between Adams who was vice president and Jefferson. Washington had long conversations with Leven about the choice he'd have to make. Washington simply didn't trust Jefferson. Leven kept sounding out Burr on what would happen if Leven, a full-blooded Virginian, would vote to put a man from Massachusetts in the White House over another Virginian."

Dorothy and Nancy looked at each other. Dorothy said, "Burr might have written long letters, but they really didn't sway Mr. Leven. It was Washington. Mr. Leven didn't know Jefferson personally, but if Washington had doubts about him, Leven wasn't going to argue about it. In a way, Leven put Adams in as president. He was the only Virginian to vote for Adams in the electoral college. He always said he voted that way because his community, Middleburg, was for Washington and the Federalists and Adams was the Federalist. He voted the way he thought his people wanted him to vote."

Jane continued, "But Father ran for Congress in 1796. Was he in the Congress when Jefferson and Aaron Burr tied in electoral votes and the election went into the House of Representatives?"

Sally said, "Yes and he wrote to our Burr at length about that, too. Over time, he developed a strong dislike for Jefferson. He thought Jefferson was deceitful and that he would say one thing but do another. He also thought Jefferson showed little respect for the Constitution and that as president he would do as he liked, no matter what the laws required. But in the end, a deal was made. Aaron Burr asked the members of the House to vote for Jefferson as president with himself as vice president. We all expected that Aaron Burr would become president after serving as vice president."

Jane said, "So Father wasn't surprised that Jefferson used armed men to chase down Aaron Burr?"

Sally said, "Nobody was surprised at that. The surprise came when the Chief Justice, John Marshall, a cousin to Jefferson, went to Richmond to preside over Aaron Burr's trial for treason. Marshall had already established the role of the Supreme Court as the main interpreter of the Constitution. When Marshall's trial found Burr innocent of all charges, Jefferson must have been angry. He and Marshall never got along, either before or after the trial. Burr was smart to leave the country for his own safety."

CHAPTER 12

JANE DECIDES TO VISIT CUTHBERT

AFTER DINNER, JANE helped her mother get ready for bed. Nancy and Dorothy, who normally went to their homes by late afternoon, had decided to stay with Sally until they heard news from the Black Eagle. They shared a cup of tea with Sally and then moved to the boys' bedroom at the rear of the large farmhouse, a relatively large room holding two beds.

Long ago, the room had provided sleeping space for four boys and three dogs. It was sparsely furnished with two small dressers under a window that looked out to the vegetable garden. The rest of the room held the two beds, leaving little floor space. The women had more than enough room for their personal belongings in the dressers and they'd done this many times before. They went to bed early, before night and full darkness.

Sally had not taken the news of Leven's death well. She tried not to show her sorrow and feelings of loss, but she'd found the visits of children and grandchildren tiring. Now that they'd gone, she didn't eat much. She lacked energy for physical tasks. She often needed help getting up out of a chair. At sixty-eight, she'd seen her share of children's illnesses and deaths. Now she believed she likely didn't have much longer in this world. She was grateful for the company of Nancy and Dorothy and glad they'd decided to stay awhile.

She said to Jane, "Well, now I have grown grandchildren to worry about."

Jane smiled as she helped her mother into bed. "It's the lucky grandmother who gets to worry about grown grandchildren," she countered "No worries about children anymore?"

Sally looked at her oldest daughter. "I don't worry about Billy. He always manages to take care of himself. But I care much about you. What will you do when I'm gone?"

Jane was surprised at her mother's directness. She replied, "You're not really ready to leave us, are you, Mother? You needn't worry about me. I'll have my teaching. Maybe I'll work on something with Father's papers. I'll keep myself busy."

"But Burr will inherit this house and land and move one of his children into it. Where would you stay? Have you thought about it?"

Jane shrugged, "I thought to go to Alexandria and buy a little house not far from Cuthbert. Alexandria is a fine city now with schools, a courthouse and lots of taverns and meeting places."

Sally tried to take a deep breath but coughed instead. She said, "Don't wait too long. Take some hams to Cuthbert and talk to him. He's always been my best boy, with a good heart. He'll try to do what's best. Alexandria would be a fine place for you. It's growing and needs teachers."

"Why do you say he's the best boy? Burr was the one who pleased Father. Most of Father's letters are to Burr. He wrote only a few to Cuthbert and none to Billy. Why didn't Father write to Billy? He was oldest." Jane was remembering the documents she'd been trying to assemble.

Sally smiled. "You were like a mother to the three of them. I don't need to tell you. Father didn't write to Billy because Billy would never have returned the favor. He was always off on some project, something that would push the boundaries of wherever he was. Father may not have written him long letters, but he left him his warrants."

Jane, curious and confused, asked, "Billy got all of them? But that was payment for Father's services in the war, a great fortune to Father. He left none of the warrants to anyone else? Not even Cuthbert?"

"No, Billy got all of it, the rights to more than six thousand acres along the Ohio. After the revolution, the Congress had no way of paying veterans of the war, so it issued warrants for land. We always thought that Washington made sure Father received a fair payment."

Sally began to remember hard times. She said, "After the revolution, there was no money anywhere. We lived by barter, trading flour and use of the mill for whatever we needed. At least now we have some dollars that mean something. Leven always credited Washington and Hamilton for settling things down after the war, but it wasn't easy. The country saw plenty of food riots and rebellions, some led by veterans who felt they had nothing to lose. Many of them went out to Ohio and settled there, using their warrants."

Jane sat by her mother's bedside and held the old woman's hand. She said, "Yes, I remember. We traded for everything and had almost nothing. But the ordinary did well. Lots of people moved west, especially the veterans. When did Billy get the warrants?"

"Oh, Father held them for a few years and then decided he wasn't going to leave Middleburg. He'd built his home here. He hoped that Billy and his friend George Morgan White Eyes would go west together and settle down. Father gave Billy the warrants around the time Aaron Burr took his group out west to explore the land Jefferson had bought. George Morgan White Eyes had family along the Ohio and Billy went with him to explore the land. I remember they were going to follow the river west. Ask Cuthbert. He probably knows about it. Maybe that's where Billy's heading now."

"Did Billy do anything about the land? Did he claim the land legally?"

"Cuthbert can tell you more than I can. I think Billy is technically the owner, but all sorts of thieves and criminals have tried to seize the warrants from veterans and their heirs, reselling them to large contracting companies. Washington and Ben Franklin were both heavily invested in companies settling Ohio."

Jane remembered that George Morgan White Eyes was a graduate of the College of New Jersey. He'd admired and worked with Aaron Burr, another College of New Jersey graduate. He'd worked for Burr when he was vice president, at a time when everyone expected that Aaron Burr would be the next president. After all, Burr had made a deal with Jefferson in 1800 when they were tied in votes in the electoral college. But after Burr killed Hamilton in a duel in 1804, Jefferson replaced him as vice president and Burr's future was bleak. He also had a new powerful enemy in Jefferson. Burr then decided to put together a party to see the new western lands and George Morgan White Eyes went with him.

Jane and George had often talked about the excitement of opening and settling new country, much as her parents had. Sorrowfully, she recalled that she and George talked about many things and they'd come close to planning a future together.

Jane reminisced about Aaron Burr. She thought that something about him was wonderful—he remained idealistic and true to principles. He meant it when he said women should vote, that everyone who works should vote, and slavery should be abolished. Burr's principles had terrified Hamilton, who believed in a strong central government. Hamilton had been a banker, related to the New York wealthy. He'd manipulated the press in New York to denounce Burr, something that led to his duel with Burr.

Jane also remembered the politics of the time. Hamilton and Jefferson, though of different parties, both feared what would happen to them personally and the country if Aaron Burr ever became president. After all, Jefferson fancied himself as a kind of Virginia landed aristocrat and opposed freeing slaves. Hamilton feared that extending the vote to large masses of working people, as Burr proposed, would lead to radical government that couldn't be controlled.

Jane smiled to herself as she remembered Aaron Burr fondly. She remembered dancing with him as a child at Valley Forge. She knew her father distrusted Jefferson though he never understood Burr. But he'd felt Burr was a comrade in arms. They knew each other from Valley Forge and Burr had fought at Quebec and Monmouth Courthouse. Jefferson had spent all that time in France, and Jane knew that Leven always believed that Jefferson admired European aristocrats and despots.

Jefferson never publicly denounced Burr, but he accused him of being a traitor and sent out a band of military men to arrest him. George Morgan White Eyes was with Burr when he was arrested in 1806. As Sally had reminded her, Burr's trial on grounds of treason took place in Richmond, ending with his acquittal, John Marshall presiding. After the trial, Burr left the country for Europe, but some of the people who'd accompanied him on his journey west had since disappeared. Nearly five years had elapsed since Burr's trial and Jane had heard nothing from George Morgan White Eyes. She thought he was dead, murdered on the way west, as Jefferson likely wanted to do to Burr.

Jane told her mother, "All right, I'll do as you suggest. I'll go see Cuthbert. I'll take two hams and the essay about Father. Don't worry too much about the grandchildren. Burr's a good father and will see to their safety. Nancy and Dorothy will be here until I return from Alexandria."

Sally smiled, showing relief. She said, "Take Edward. We won't need him around the house and I'm sure he'd like to visit some of his family in Alexandria. Don't waste time. Cuthbert might be able to help with finding Billy, or at least in dealing with the cutthroats who are after him."

CHAPTER 13

THE ROAD TO ALEXANDRIA

EDWARD, SALLY'S HOUSE servant, was over seventy years old, but he was still good with horses. He'd worked for the Powell family almost all his life. A black man, he was born free and his family, also free, owned property they farmed west of Middleburg. Jane always enjoyed his company and he'd been a great help to her when, as a youngster, she'd had the responsibility for Billy, Burr and Cuthbert.

Early on a Wednesday morning, Edward and Jane arranged themselves in a buggy, with Jane up front next to Edward and the packages for Cuthbert tied down on the small back seat. Jane carried Edward's rifle in her lap, mainly because she knew she was a better shot than Edward, whose eyes were failing.

Jane whistled to the black horse, who jumped around with excitement. The horse was young and strong, and Edward said, "Miss Jane, he doesn't need encouragement. He'll get us to Alexandria before dark."

Jane laughed. She was delighted to be out and away on a beautiful spring morning. She worried a bit for her mother but knew that Nancy and Dorothy would be there to help if anything should happen. She said to Edward, "We're getting on in years, aren't we? And still worrying about what's happening with Billy."

"Miss Jane, you're not old. You've spent too much of your life worrying over Billy. He can take care of himself."

"Do you really think so? He's always had us to look out for him and he's always known it."

"He thinks like your daddy. He knows where he wants to go, though he's not sure what he'll do when he gets there."

"Well, it looks like he's on his way to Ohio, taking a Bible and a few guns and being followed by some violent thugs who claim he owes them something."

"Your daddy started out the same way. He didn't just buy the ordinary, you know. We had a good solid gunfight with people who'd moved into the place in the beginning. Your dad bought the place all right, but vagrants and criminals had to be pushed out. Two of your mama's brothers came out with some friends from an eastern Virginia militia to help. They all ended up staying here. There'd be no Middleburg without that fight. It would have stayed a lawless wasteland."

Jane looked at Edward. "Well, I guess history is all about the work of people determined to get ahead. I don't remember my father talking about a fight for the ordinary, but we always had to be armed and able to shoot." Jane thought about her essay and said, "He always supported the militia and was quick to volunteer for anything that involved keeping law and order. You're right about Billy there; he was always ready to be going somewhere."

The spring sun shone brilliantly and the countryside had sprung to life with vivid greens in the trees and wildflowers popping up through the brush. Birds sang loudly and the day warmed. Edward kept the young horse going for three hours, passing several wagons going in the opposite direction. In a wide part of the dirt road, they pulled over to a small clearing to see the goods in a parked tinker's wagon. The driver had unhitched his horse to give it a rest and the wagon carried some iron pots and finer stuff made of copper. Jane talked to the driver, who worked for a blacksmith in Leesburg. From him, she bought her mother a gift of a copper kettle and a copper frying pan for Cuthbert.

After midday, they stopped near a creek where the horse could rest and have some water and they could have something to eat. While Edward unhitched the horse and led him by a rope down to the creek's edge, tying him to a small tree, Jane spread out a blanket and opened a basket of fruit, dried meat, cheese and bread baked the previous evening. The horse calmed down and was pleased to drink and rest in the shade near the bubbling creek.

After they'd eaten, Jane asked, "Edward, what did you think of Washington? What does your family think of him?" She still thought about her essay and Edward had been around during the whole of her father's life. Edward was father of six and grandfather to twenty-two. Two of his sons had gone west, though his oldest son still farmed the family land outside Middleburg. His daughters had married various tradesmen around the area.

"Well, your father admired him greatly and I respected his opinion. For me, I never knew whether Washington was the great leader in war, though my children believe that. They love anyone they can imagine astride a great horse. For me, he really became great when he was the leader in peace. Washington was for growth and law and order and he showed his principles when he freed his slaves in his will. That was a great thing for a Virginia planter to do. Principles meant something to Washington."

"My father was the same. Of course, with his Quaker background, we never kept slaves. Father never had doubts about supporting independence and the Constitution, and I think his love for Washington was part of that. But he didn't just follow the leader. He really believed and fought for what he thought was a life of freedom for his family."

Edward smiled at Jane. "Not just freedom, Miss Jane. The men who followed Washington wanted to open the country and settle it. Washington was a surveyor when he was young. He'd been to Pennsylvania and Ohio. He owned a lot of land in Ohio himself."

Jane looked at Edward and asked, "You know about Father's warrants?"

Edward stared at Jane and said, "Back to Billy. You'll need to talk to Mr. Cuthbert about that."

They packed up their picnic, washed their hands in the creek and hitched the horse to the buggy. They arrived at Cuthbert's house in Alexandria before dark.

Cuthbert lived in a two-story red brick house across the street from a spacious market square. He'd lived in Alexandria since the end of the revolution and the city was the major port on the Potomac. Flour, wheat and other goods were shipped to foreign places from Alexandria and the city hosted numerous foreign ships bringing wines, rum, coffee and manufactured goods from many countries. Alexandria thrived as the largest city in Virginia with a population of over seven thousand. Its streets teemed with industrious young people out to make fortunes for themselves.

Washington's home, Mount Vernon, was situated near Alexandria, a part of the large parcel of land Washington had owned along the Potomac. Washington had willingly donated the land for the capital city and had never lobbied to make Alexandria the seat of national government. When Washington's slaves were freed, many of them settled in Alexandria. By 1810, a little more than ten years after Washington's death, the city's people included a diverse population, including free blacks and a large community of Quakers.

Alexandria's market square, taverns and theaters drew people from far and wide. The town provided lavish entertainments for presidents Adams, Jefferson and Madison, as Washington City on the other side of the river was mostly undeveloped and the White House remained an isolated structure on the edge of a swamp.

Under the provisions of the District of Columbia Act passed by the new congress in 1791, Alexandria became part of the new District of Columbia. A charter passed by the congress divided Alexandria into four wards to be governed by a sixteen-member council. Cuthbert, an elected member of the council and its presiding officer, decided to keep the title of "mayor," a traditional title in Alexandria.

When they arrived, the bright blue sky was beginning to darken. Two of Cuthbert's servants came out to help Jane out of the buggy. They also unpacked the back seat holding Cuthbert's packages and Jane's small and lightweight leather traveling trunk. Cuthbert watched the unloading with two of his daughters and shouted, "What a wonderful surprise!! Are you here for my birthday? That was last week but you're still welcome."

Jane smiled at Cuthbert and realized he'd always been her favorite, always happy with a smile on his face. Now he lived in the largest town in Virginia, served as mayor and lived in a fine waterfront townhouse with his wife and ten children. Jane looked at her tall, thin younger brother and said, "Yes, I brought you a proper frying pan."

Cuthbert's two daughters giggled when they heard that. Jane climbed the three front steps of the brick house and embraced the girls. Cuthbert, with a big smile on his face, said, "You can't take us by surprise. We're ready for you any time you want to come."

The girls ushered Jane inside and told her she would be sleeping with three of them, ages six, eight and ten. They occupied a small room with a very large bed. The room had a large window which faced the river and the Alexandria docks.

When Jane went inside, Cuthbert called to Edward, who tipped his hat and said he would take the buggy to his cousin five streets away, where he'd stay until Jane needed him to return. Cuthbert approached the buggy and asked Edward, "Is there anything you can tell me about this visit?"

Edward smiled, "She loves you and Billy and Burr, but her mama wants some settlement about the warrants and George Morgan White Eyes. She's here because she was told to come. Make believe she's Washington on his white horse. Show some respect." With that, he rode away.

CHAPTER 14
CUTHBERT AND JANE TALK

A FTER THE DAY'S journey, Jane, though weary, wanted a walk and some fresh air. Cuthbert suggested they go down to the docks where they could watch the ships, large ones anchored in deep water and small boats meandering in and out or tied to posts. The harbor, darkening quickly as daylight faded, still had the hum of activity from the loading and unloading of barrels and crates. The sounds seemed gay, even joyous.

They walked a half-mile and found a tree stump on which they sat. Jane said, "How lovely! How is it that of all the Powells you were the only one to find a place in a town? All the rest of us look to the west, and you went east."

Cuthbert laughed and then lit up a small clay pipe. He said, "That's the price one pays for education, and you put me up for that. The schools are in the old places and if you want to study anything, you have to go east, or worse, even Europe."

Jane replied, "Yes. I remember the arguments we had when you announced you wanted to study. Father never appreciated the need for higher education and Mother didn't want you to go to William and Mary. I talked to her at length about it, because I was all for you going to a college. You remember? I taught you to read."

"Of course I remember, and to write. I owe my flowing mayor's handwriting to you."

Jane reminisced, "Though William and Mary was the only college in Virginia, Mother thought it was a place for rich planters' children. Jefferson studied there along with a lot of other people from slave-holding families. Both Mother and Father were strongly against holding slaves. They were pleased when Congress decided that the new Northwest Territory would have no slavery. I think that's part of the reason they looked to the west."

Cuthbert interrupted her thought with his own recollections. He said, "I remember that Father wasn't clear about the need for formal education, but he didn't oppose William and Mary. He argued that Washington favored William and Mary because he got his surveyor's certificate there."

Jane replied, "Mother just smirked at that and said that Washington was a great man, not just a surveyor, and that William and Mary was lucky to have him, not the other way around. You were clever to mention George Morgan White Eyes. That got them to relent a bit. At least you got a year out of it, though not in Virginia. Are you happy that you went to the College of New Jersey for that one year? It took some pushing from me and Anne before Mother agreed to it. Father eventually just went along with the idea."

"Of course! I enjoyed the college, more for the friends I made than what I learned. Billy and George were long gone by the time I went there. You're right about Father. He never saw the need for philosophy. He thought that if you wanted to get from point A to point B without too much difficulty, you'd better build a good road."

Jane laughed at that. "Yes, he was proud of his east-west turnpike. Burr rides on it right now as we speak; Father's own toll road legislated by Congress. That's how Middleburg got its name.

Town for the village, but he refused. He suggested Middleburg, for being halfway between Alexandria and Winchester. I think he had an idea for the highway when he bought the ordinary."

They both sat comfortably, but Cuthbert knew Jane well. When she did her daily chores, she energetically moved about and walked. She sat only when she was tired. He said, "Let's go home. We have things to talk about, but they'll keep till tomorrow when we're both fresh." They walked back slowly, each thinking of what to say in the morning.

The next day began with a light spring rain. Jane slept soundly, even while sharing a soft bed with three giggling nieces. As usual, she rose with the first hint of daylight, well before any of the children woke. She dressed and went down to the large kitchen where Molly, the family cook, prepared a large pot of porridge for breakfast. The porridge pot hung on a hook suspended over the large wood-burning kitchen hearth.

Jane brought out her essay and laid it on a small table under a window not far from the hearth. Little natural light made it through the window that morning and Jane could barely make out what she'd written. She looked up and asked Molly, "Could I have a cup of tea, please?"

Molly gestured to a large copper teapot being warmed on a second hook suspended over the hearth, while she continued stirring the porridge. She said, "Please help yourself. I think the water is warm enough. The tea is on the shelf behind you. Would you like some porridge? Some biscuits and jam? We have some raspberry preserves."

Jane found teacups on a small shelf hanging on a wall near the table. She took the teapot and placed it on the table. She then spooned some tea into the teapot's steeping tray and placed the tray in the teapot. After a few minutes, she poured herself a cup of tea, saying, "Oh, save the porridge for the children. I'll have a biscuit and jam for now."

Molly laughed, "The children? This is mainly for Mr. Cuthbert who has the same breakfast every morning. I thought you might be the same."

"Not me. I look for some variety. I'd love to try the preserves. Where do you keep them?"

Molly motioned to a small cupboard on the wall opposite the window. At that moment, Cuthbert entered the kitchen. He said, "I heard that! Trying our preserves is definitely not an act of bravery. You'll want to bring some back to Mother."

He looked at Jane with eyelids so droopy they seemed to cover his nose down to his moustache. He clearly was not used to being up so early. Looking at him, Jane said imperiously, "Sit down and join me for a cup of tea, please." With that, she put her cup in his hand, put her arm on his shoulder, and guided him to a chair at the table where she'd left the essay. Molly giggled at the sight of him wobbling into the chair. Jane poured herself another cup of tea and replaced the teapot, still steeping the tea, on its hook over the hearth.

Cuthbert smiled at his sister who all his life had been more like a mother to him than a sister. He said, "You brought me a frying pan. Do you mean to whack me with it? Why?" With that, he sipped the tea and slowly gained his strength and focus. He also noticed Jane's essay on the table but said nothing about it.

Jane sat down at the table and tried some of the preserves. She handed Cuthbert a biscuit slathered with the raspberry concoction that clearly contained more than a little rum. She said, "The preserves are wonderful, but go slow with that so early in the day, I think. I suppose you'll want some porridge as well."

Cuthbert motioned to Molly, who spooned out a bowl of porridge and placed a decanter of cream on the table. She then moved the porridge pot onto a smaller hook away from the hearth's high flames, so the porridge would stay warm and not cook rapidly. She then left the kitchen.

Cuthbert took Jane's hand and looked at her. He said, "Why worry? You're here for a holiday and I'm here to please you. I see you've been working." He held up the essay.

Jane remarked, "Yes, we've passed through Valley Forge and gotten to 1796 and Jefferson. That brought us to a conversation about George Morgan White Eyes and Aaron Burr. Our conversations became muddy, and Mother became anxious over Billy and grandchildren we sent out for news of him, namely Burr and his John and Beth. I needed a rest from all the worry. I thought you might be able to explain a few things more fully than Father's letters. You're welcome to look at what I've written so far."

"Is that all? We have lots to sort out. By the way, how is Mother keeping?"

"Not well. Sorrow has overcome her, and she feels her age. She actually sent me here to talk to you about my future, no less."

"I had a notion of something like that. Mother and I haven't spoken, but you know you'll always be welcome in my home. If you like I can find you a house nearby, big enough to take in some students. You could have your own little school for young people."

"You've already thought about this? Did Mother put you up to it? Did Burr?"

"You always imagine a conspiracy. Of course not. I've always had an eye out for you, just as you have for me and the other boys. In fact, it was Billy who suggested I start thinking about it. I spoke to him at length when he was here in Alexandria, before he took off for the west. You know Burr. He thinks of Burr and only Burr, and possibly his children. I'm surprised he took both John and Beth with him."

Jane took a sip of the tea, and then said, "Beth had to make a fuss for him to take her and she's met up with other youngsters at Logan's on the way to the Black Eagle. She's the real Powell; loves the idea of going through the woods to look for Billy, making her way west. John didn't say much but seemed to be trying to please his father more than looking forward to an adventure. He's not a talkative boy. Last I heard, Burr and John were traveling the main road. Beth and a few other youngsters made it to Logan's and from there are following a shortcut to the Black Eagle. They should all arrive about the same time. We know nothing about where Billy might be."

Cuthbert enjoyed the biscuit and fresh preserves and moved on to the bowl of porridge. He said nothing but started reading Jane's essay.

Jane stood up to warm her hands at the hearth, came back to the table, sat down and said, "Well, let's start at the beginning then. Tell me about Billy and your conversations with him. Mother had him in mind when she suggested I speak to you. She mentioned something about Father's land warrants."

Cuthbert coughed when he heard this.

CHAPTER 15
LAND WARRANTS

CUTHBERT READ JANE'S essay and thought a moment before he spoke. He said, "I remember this letter of Father's describing his illness at Valley Forge. Have you ever thought about how fortunate our family has been? Through war, illness, gunfights in the town? So many of us are still here to remember it. Mother has grown grandchildren. Father saw his village and toll road built."

Jane responded, "Yes, our family has come a long way, but no use looking back. We need to see forward. Where will the children go and what will they do? The essay is just gibberish unless we add something of our own beliefs to it."

Cuthbert took the essay and read further. Finally, he said, "Some of us would rather do things than write and read about it. What you do reflects what you believe. You know that."

"Yes, stop being mysterious. Tell me about Billy. What's he up to now?"

"I hope you'll keep some of this to yourself. No use adding to Mother's worries."

"That much to worry about?"

"Yes. I'll begin with the warrants. Father signed all of them over to Billy, rights to about six thousand acres along the Ohio, not far from the new town of Cincinnati. The town was built by veterans of the war and they named it, in their own way, for Washington. Cincinnatus was a Roman hero and farmer who saved the Roman Republic and then returned to his farm, much the way Washington did."

"Has Billy registered his claims legally? Has he seen the land?"

"He went out to see the property a few years ago. He went west just before Aaron Burr and his party went out to see the new lands bought by Jefferson from the French. George Morgan White Eyes started out with Burr. When Burr's party went south, George decided to stay in Ohio where he had family. George and Billy found each other and agreed to farm some of Billy's land and build a business or two and ports along the river. They had some grand plans."

Jane was confused. She asked, "But Billy came back. Did he leave his warrants with George? Did he trade them for deeds to the property legally sealed?"

"There was no authority accessible in Ohio to draw up the deeds. This was 1805 and Ohio had been a state for only two years. Billy stayed on his property awhile, started a few businesses, and came back last year to complete the transaction in a federal court."

"All sounds so normal and methodical for Billy."

"I think you're seeing the influence of George."

Jane became wistful. She asked, "Tell me about George; is he keeping well? When I heard his parents were murdered by an army thug, I thought he died as well. I haven't heard from him in five years."

"He's alive and well and planning to come back and see you. Do you have an interest?"

Jane stood up and walked to the hearth. She felt her heart heaving and soon began to weep. Cuthbert sat quietly and soon stood up to go to his sister. He put his arm around her and said, "I know this is a surprise. Let's take this slowly. George cares for you and wants you to share his life. I'm afraid this story becomes even more complicated."

"I can take complication. People coming back from the dead is another story."

"You know I have this secondhand from Billy. George went to Ohio where he had family. His father had been a chief of the Lenape and his mother English, and George had aunts, uncles and cousins in southern Ohio. George's parents were traveling to Ohio when they were murdered by a scout working for the army. Nobody really knows anything about that scout or who sent him. At the time, George was working for Aaron Burr, who was vice president. The previous year, Burr had killed Hamilton in a duel, and Jefferson had decided to dump Burr as his vice president. This, of course, violated the deal he'd made with Burr in 1800.

"Aaron Burr had enemies everywhere. When George found his cousins, they welcomed him, but he'd been tracked by army thugs working for Jefferson. Jefferson's soldiers had orders to kill George. Jefferson wanted anyone who had ever worked for Aaron Burr eliminated."

"So, this is also politics?"

"Politics is everywhere you look. No getting away from it. The thugs Jefferson sent out worked for money, but they had no trouble killing anyone with dark skin. Luckily for George, the Ohio Indians who took him in knew how to handle their defense. You know, once you leave Middleburg and Winchester, the country still belongs to the tribes. Ohio is a large state but very sparsely settled in some regions. Anyway, the Indians fought off a raiding party aimed at killing George and protected him. In return, he took an Indian wife who a year later gave him a son. His wife died in the process."

"Oh, dear. What about Billy in all this?"

"Billy came back to Virginia more than a year ago. He was flush with cash from his Ohio businesses and had set about putting together a wagon train of settlers who would come out to Cincinnati and settle there. He met up with the Johnstons. You remember them? Their son-in-law John Simpson agreed to invest in Billy's businesses. He planned to take his family west."

"Yes, we had a visit from George and Mary Johnston not long ago. They warned us about a man named Jack Walsh."

Cuthbert eyed Jane. "How much do you know about Jack Walsh?"

"Nothing. He sounded like a hired killer who had some claim against Billy."

"Well, this is how it is. Billy and I had the warrants. We took them to the federal court here and exchanged them for property deeds that must be countersigned by a court in Chillicothe, Ohio's capital city. The deeds are made out to Billy and the completion of the transaction is just a formality."

"So, what does this have to do with Jack Walsh?"

"As I understand it, Jack Walsh is currently working for a large land speculation company, the Transylvania Company. They own huge parcels of land in Kentucky and Ohio. It's his job to buy out warrants from veterans who don't plan to move west. When he heard about Billy's warrants, he made him an offer, which Billy refused. Simpson, though, owed Walsh from a previous event and now was Billy's partner. On that basis, Walsh demanded payment from Billy, in the form of the warrants. Simpson's debt to Walsh comes from some land-based business deal made a few years ago, all spelled out in complicated contracts. Walsh may be able to use his position with the Transylvania Company to use their high-priced lawyers. Walsh, being who he is, will kill to get his way."

Jane paced around the kitchen. She asked indignantly, "Can someone just kill a party to get his property?"

"The lawyers will muddy the property rights. The Transylvania Company is such a large landowner that it would likely prevail in court if a dispute ever got there. That's why our Burr is so anxious to get to Billy."

"What does this have to do with our Burr and his children?"

"He believes that Father's warrants belong to the family and are meant for Virginians. Billy doesn't live in Virginia any more. Burr wants Billy to take his son, John Powell, as a partner. Then Burr will sponsor legislation in the Virginia General Assembly to protect the transaction."

"Is that what a General Assembly is for? To protect Burr's private property rights? To protect the property of the members of the General Assembly? Washington would turn in his grave to hear this. Mr. Madison, our president, wouldn't like it much either. Maybe we should add a chapter to Father's essay showing how far the Powell children have strayed from Leven's vision of justice."

"I told you that politics is everywhere and it's not really a clean business. Remember, the General Assembly would be noticed by the Transylvania Company. The company has substantial assets in Virginia. For Transylvania, six thousand acres in Ohio likely doesn't counterbalance what they own in southern and western Virginia. The General Assembly could persuade them with the threat of a nasty tax law."

Jane took a deep breath and looked at the ceiling. She then looked at Cuthbert and asked, "So, what's next? What will you do to help your brother Billy?"

"Funny you should ask. To start, I've already asked the federal authorities here in Alexandria to apprehend Mr. Jack Walsh on charges of fraud and theft. He apparently had some success bilking other families in the town. This is a personal charge against Walsh himself, not the Transylvania Company. Since we know that Billy is heading west, a team of four federal agents set out for Middleburg and Winchester just yesterday, fully armed with arrest warrants, guns and ammunition. Will that do?"

"Will they get there in time to do anything?"

Cuthbert shrugged at the question. He stood, posed as he often did when he gave a speech, with a finger pointed in the air, and announced, "I've also, as Mayor of Alexandria, asked the president of the Transylvania Company, a Mr. Richard Anderson, who fought in the war and knew Daniel Boone, to consider the matter. He comes to Alexandria from time to time and has a house on the next street. I've asked him to call back Jack Walsh and talk to him."

"What do you think that will do?"

"I don't know. Walsh is nobody's idea of a loyal employee. Walsh could just try to take the property for himself and make off with it. A thug is a thug, after all."

Jane said nothing. She sat down and sipped her tea as four of Cuthbert's children filled the adjoining dining room and waited for breakfast.

PART TWO

INDIAN COUNTRY AND WINCHESTER

CHAPTER 16

THE ROAD TO
INDIAN COUNTRY

BOBBY AND DANIEL asked for fast horses but were allowed only the two their fathers would spare. They were older steeds with sweet temperaments and accustomed to the boys. The boys also listened to lectures from their parents. They were to listen for unusual sounds and make note of their surroundings. They were not to shoot first at every strange noise and to beware of thieves and mother bears. Finally, they were to deliver the Powell message to the Black Eagle where they were to ask for Dorothy's cousin Henry Silver. They were told to be polite and ask for news of Billy.

Bobby, a tall, stringy boy of fifteen who wore his dark brown hair tied behind his neck, immediately told Daniel that this time Bobby would be leader of their party, because he was eight months older and a foot taller.

Daniel responded, "Well, if you have to be the leader, find a dog. You won't get me."

"My father says I can't go by myself. We have to go almost to Winchester and part of the road is through mountains and woods."

"So, Mr. Leader, why do you think I'm supposed to go? You'd get lost in a forest of two trees and never remember your way back."

"I know. You track better than I do, but you'd be no good against a black bear. Also, I'll be better at delivering the message and remembering what they tell us about Billy. Besides, I'm the cousin to Henry Silver."

Daniel, short and stocky, with a pleasant, round face and straight black hair down to his shoulders, considered the best way to proceed. He said, "I can shoot straight enough, but I wouldn't go myself. I'd take my sister Susan. She's got a good brain for the woods and she can shoot."

To Bobby and Daniel, adding another good tracker and an extra shot wasn't a bad idea for a long expedition. Susan, thirteen, was a pretty girl who tied her black, curly hair behind her head with a ribbon. Though smaller than the boys, she was quick and athletic and far more perceptive than either of them. The boys, who often argued with her over almost everything, still generally included her and her dog Prince in short hunting expeditions.

Bobby asked, "Do you think we should ask her if she'd like to go? Prince would be great on a trip like this."

By the time they started, the party included the three teenagers, three mild farm horses that were good at carrying loads uphill, a mule named King George carrying supplies, and Prince, a lively beagle who'd been on a few duck hunts. The teenagers packed pistols and rifles, and the mule carried enough food for three days.

When Dorothy told Sally and Nancy about the preparations, the three grandmothers shared other memories of making tracks through dark woods full of wild animals amid general warfare and mayhem.

Sally wondered, "Have we made no progress since then? Are they better equipped than we were?"

Nancy, Daniel's grandmother, said, "Of course! They're better equipped and they know more than we knew. Bob and I had an old mule and five dollars. I wasn't much use with weapons and the woods frightened me. We stuck to traveled paths. The children have all hunted, been to the woods, know what they're up against. Good for Daniel to ask Susan; that shows common sense, though I think now they'll have many more arguments along the way."

Dorothy said, "Yes, and that's good for their education too. Nothing's better than dealing with differences of opinion when you're facing something new. Don't you wish you were a fly in King George's ear right now?"

Jane laughed at that. "Do you remember White Marsh? I have a letter or two from that time. What do you remember of it?"

Sally thought and said, "Leven went to White Marsh late in the year. He'd come home for a while and spent a good part of the year with us. He was in Virginia when Congress finally declared independence and appointed Washington as Commander of the Continental Army. Before independence, Leven was a major in the Loudoun militia. In January 1777, he became a lieutenant colonel of the Sixteenth Regiment of Virginia Continentals. He was so proud of that and thought Washington remembered him and was somehow responsible for his rank. He left for White Marsh in the fall. Winter came early and was severe."

Nancy said, "We were in a real war by then. Philadelphia was where the Continental Congress met and it was an early British target. The City of Brotherly Love had plenty of Tories. Washington's army went to protect our new capital from attack."

Jane vaguely remembered White Marsh but couldn't quite place any event there. She would have been about seven years old when Leven wrote:

"Camp at White Marsh Church, 11 miles above Phila., Nov. 7, 1777.

"My dear—As I cannot omit any opportunity of writing you, I make use of this to inform you, first, that I am well, and second, that an affair happened the day before yesterday that not only does great honor to the American armies, but in my opinion it will be of infinite importance in its consequences.

"... It seems the enemy made a vigorous effort, but was repulsed three different times ... provisions are extremely scarce and bad and I have not much doubt but the enemy must go ... It is a great misfortune that we have not more men; 10,000 more would have finished the war some time since without fighting. The Militia will not do; they are restless, cannot wait in Camp. ...

"General Clinton has evacuated Ft. Montgomerie and burned everything on the shores of the North River, secured himself again in New York.

"Having bad conveniences for writing and a crowd around me in a small Tent, I must conclude.

"Sincerely, your loving husband, Leven Powell

"I hope to have the pleasure of seeing you this winter."

"Yes, I remember that one," Sally said. "We immediately began planning a trip to Leven's camp. Soon after that letter arrived, we heard that the British had marched into Philadelphia. Many of our people fled and took what they could with them. They even took the Liberty Bell, so the British couldn't melt it down for bullets. Just a few weeks later, we won the battle of Saratoga. Washington didn't know at the time, but the French would come to the rescue by spring. With Philadelphia in British hands, Washington set up his winter camp at Valley Forge and Lady Washington accompanied him. Leven and the other officers asked family to come spend Christmas up there. Lady Washington planned to entertain the officers and their wives."

Jane said, "I remember the coach ride up to Valley Forge. Billy, Burr and me with Nancy and you and quite a lot of packages."

Nancy laughed. "Packages? They were mostly hams to leave with Leven. We also brought books. He needed a way to spend the time."

Jane remembered, "Yes, we loved sleeping in a big tent with the fire outside. The officers and soldiers were very kind. We had a few dozen children in our tent during the day."

Nancy remembered well. "Well over thirty, all under twelve. Billy was eleven and annoyed to be grouped with the younger set. Your father made sure to bring him over to meet Washington. He was so excited; he was introduced to General and Lady Washington, but mostly he struck up a conversation with one of the general's aides, Mr. Burr."

Sally said, "That's right. Aaron Burr was a young man of about twenty. He was small, but quite a handsome and well-spoken fellow. Many ladies hovered around him. Several afternoons he came down to the children's tent with a flutist and mandolin player. He organized dances and made sure to dance with every young girl."

Jane exclaimed, "I'll never forget that! He was in his uniform and I thought him spectacular. Mainly, he was lively and could not stop talking about how people should have their own country. He took time with all the girls as well as the boys. Billy was very impressed; Burr less so."

Sally asked, "Why so?"

"Well, Mr. Burr made a great event out of Burr's first name being the same as his last name. Mr. Burr commented that they must be cousins. He thought it a great joke, but our Burr was only ten and embarrassed by the whole thing."

Sally said, "Yes, Aaron Burr was very much the all-out republican. He wanted women to vote and he would have freed all the slaves. At the age of twenty, he was a graduate of the College of New Jersey, a fine public speaker, and idealistic. Many people thought he'd have a great future."

Dorothy and Nancy looked at each other and Jane knew their

meaning. She said, "No need to jump ahead of ourselves. When he was twenty, Burr was brave and beautiful and that's how we remember him. His later enemies, Jefferson and Hamilton, couldn't have been more different from him and from each other. Maybe they were right to worry about what Burr might have done as president. Father didn't worry about that at all. He always thought Burr looked to the future and cared about the country, especially ordinary citizens."

CHAPTER 17
STARTING OUT WEST

EARLY ON A sunny May morning, Bobby and Daniel rode their horses ahead of King George, the mule, who carried their bed rolls and food supplies on his back. Susan followed on a small pony while Prince, the dog, sometimes raced ahead or found something to sniff on the side of the road.

The unpaved road, well-marked with small pebbles and sticks, took them over flat grassland and low, but gradually rising hills. Lightly leaved clumps of trees shaded them part of the way and they could hear running water from nearby creeks.

The two boys riding together spoke quietly, mainly of hunting, but the chatter of birds singing in the trees often interrupted their conversation. Susan watched for birds and animals and kept a close eye on Prince. Along the way, she spotted two foxes and signs in the brush of heavy-footed travelers who'd recently preceded them.

That first day, the boys knew where they were going. They were to stop at Logan's farm where they would deliver four hams. By early afternoon, Bobby had caught sight of the Logan farmhouse, a wooden structure with a large porch in front and a low-slung second story to the rear.

The day was going to be hot, and though the teenagers weren't tired, they were hungry and ready for a break. When Prince saw the small farmhouse, he leaped and sped ahead of the party while King George brayed loudly. Susan pulled her pony ahead of the boys, but the pony couldn't catch up to Prince. By the time the three teenagers reached the front porch, the Logan family was outside, laughing as they greeted the travelers.

Grandma Logan, a gray-haired woman of sixty, sat in a rocking chair. Prince panted and tried to leap into her lap. She shouted to Susan, "Is this your doggie, darlin'? He's a charmer I'm sure, but no watch dog."

Susan ran up the porch steps and hugged Grandma and Grandpa Logan and then said, "His name is Prince and he's to help us track our way to the Black Eagle." Prince calmed down and licked Grandma's hand.

By this time, Bobby and Daniel had dismounted. They tied King George to a hitching post and started unloading him. Then they walked up the porch steps, each carrying two hams. Bobby spoke first to Henry Logan, a tall, gaunt man of forty. "These are four hams for your summer use, my momma says."

Henry smiled and took the hams inside.

Martha Logan, the mother of the house, short and plump with red, curly hair now turning gray around the edges, smiled at them. She said, "Thank you kindly. We're pleased to see you all. Can you stay a bit?"

Bobby looked at Daniel, who quickly replied, "We have to deliver a paper message to the Black Eagle. It's a letter from Jane Powell to her brother Billy, if we can find where he is. Have you seen him or spoken to him?"

Martha, impressed with Daniel's seriousness, looked at the grandparents. Then she turned to the boys. "We know you have a job to do, but it's going to be hot today and we need to talk about the best route to the Black Eagle. Burr Powell was here just two days ago, and Beth is staying with us for now. Why don't you boys situate yourselves in the horse barn? Steve and Andrew are already sleeping out there, now that the weather's turned warm. Susan can stay here in the house with Amy and Hannah."

Grandma Logan stood up and took Susan's hand, "Where does Prince stay?"

"Usually with me. He's not much more than a baby."

"Well, you'll be sharing a bed with Amy and Hannah, and now Beth. You'll have to work it out with them."

Then they went into the house. The front door opened directly into a large kitchen and cooking hearth. A sleeping loft that held a straw bed for the boys hung over half the kitchen. Under the loft a door opened to a narrow stairwell and a downstairs bedroom where the Logans and three small children slept. The stairs led to two upstairs rooms, one holding a bed for the grandparents and another bedroom for the girls.

Susan, who'd been in the house many times before, ran through the kitchen and up the stairs to the girls' bedroom, followed by Prince. There she found Beth Powell, Amy Logan, a red-haired girl of twelve, and Hannah Logan, a blond of fourteen. The Logan girls were conversing and laughing with Beth. Susan knew Amy and Hannah from early childhood as they'd been to each other's birthday celebrations. Susan knew that Martha, the Logan girls' mother, was second cousin to Dorothy, Bobby's grandmother, and related to the owners of the Black Eagle.

Amy asked, "Why are you here?"

Prince leaped up onto the bed and sat between Amy and Beth.

"We're to deliver a message to the Black Eagle and find out where Billy Powell might be. Beth's father, Burr, is already looking for him and gone to Winchester. Has anyone been here recently?"

Hannah took Prince into her lap and the young dog licked her face. Susan lay down on the bed which now held all four girls. Susan pointed to the dog and said, "His name is Prince, and he acts like one. He does whatever he likes, whenever he feels like it."

Hannah moved Prince to the end of the bed and said, "Well, you have Prince, but we've had a lovely visit from some black bears. A magician making his way to Winchester came through over a year ago and had a big mother bear with him. He called her Louise and she climbed up and down ladders and tumbled, making us all laugh. He stayed in the barn for about two weeks, and when it was time to go he couldn't find Louise. She'd disappeared into the woods. He was worried about her and thought she wouldn't know how to feed herself. Well, this past February Louise came back to the horse barn, this time with a baby bear cub. He's the most beautiful fellow you've ever seen, black and shiny and round. Momma gave him some honey biscuits and he loved them. We named him Blackbeard, because he'll steal anything sweet if he has the chance."

"The bears are still here? Don't the boys sleep in the barn?"

"That's one of the reasons the boys are there. They're supposed to scare the bears away. The horses don't like to be near bears. Louise and the baby left a few weeks ago. Dad thinks Louise is teaching him to catch fish down near the creek and that they're living in the forest. We have quite a few black bears in the forest near here."

Prince leaped off the bed and Amy looked at him. "You'd be a great playmate for Blackbeard, don't you think?"

Hannah looked at him and said, "Tonight, you sleep on the floor." She folded an old blanket and threw it down at the foot of the bed, but Prince paid no attention.

Later that afternoon, all the assembled guests and family sat at a large table in the shade of a large oak tree. Martha began the conversation. "Tell us why you need to go to the Black Eagle."

Bobby responded, "We're carrying a message for Billy Powell who went west a week ago. His brother is out looking for him, and our grandmothers, along with old Mrs. Powell, worry about his safety. Some varmints are out to get him. My grandmother thought someone at the Black Eagle would know about whoever was around and where they might be located. We're supposed to hurry back with any information."

"Well, Burr was here two days ago. He went on ahead using the open road, taking John with him."

Henry Logan asked, "What if you find the varmints? What would you do?"

Daniel said, "We have rifles. We can use them."

Henry looked at the boys. "And you have your sister and a dog and a mule. I think it best you get to the Black Eagle as quick as you can, deliver the message, and get back to your grandmothers using the open road, also quick as you can."

Martha said, "Take one of the hams to the Black Eagle and say it's from me. Henry will show you a short way to go through the woods. It should take no more than a day."

Henry added, "You'll have to camp in the woods for one night and you'll get there by midday the next day. But you'll be on your own, maybe near varmints and black bears. You'll need to be sensible and prepared."

Beth spoke up. "I'd like to go with them. After all, Billy is my uncle and my dad and brother are out looking for him. With Susan, I'm sure I could be a help with the tracking and all."

Daniel said, "Some help! Two girls! You're going to make so much noise, the varmints and bears will know exactly where to find us."

Susan laughed, "Then go yourself. Beth and I will make it to the Black Eagle before you and King George, and we'll have a better campfire at night. You'd go hungry and cold before you could light a fire."

"Enough arguing," Martha interrupted. "The four of you can go, but Bobby, Daniel and Susan must return quickly with news for the grandmothers. Beth can decide for herself what's right after you get to the Black Eagle. Her dad might be there; they may already have seen Billy."

With that, Susan and Beth went up to bed and an all-night planning session, because Susan wanted to see the black bears. Grandma Logan had already given Beth about twelve small honey biscuits. Beth thought she could help spot them, as she'd seen bear tracks before.

Bobby and Daniel went out to the barn where they met Andrew and Steve Logan. The boys inspected their rifles. Knowing that Bobby and Daniel were about to journey through the woods, Steve Logan suggested he exchange his rifle for Bobby's. Steve told Bobby, "I hope you don't need this, but it's pretty accurate at twenty feet."

The Logan boys would have loved to go with them to the Black Eagle, but Henry Logan would have none of it. In May on a farm, there's a great deal of work to be done and the Logan boys, ages seventeen and eighteen, were needed at home. Henry prepared to guide the teenagers into the woods, but only part way. He planned to give them careful instructions as to how to find the Black Eagle from across a second creek.

CHAPTER 18

IN THE WOODS

EARLY ON A sunny morning, Henry Logan led the way into the back woods, riding his sturdy gray farm horse. The teenagers paired off with the boys behind Henry on their farm horses, followed by King George, fully packed with food and sleeping blankets. Behind the mule came the two girls on their small ponies, followed by Prince. The boys sat up in their saddles and kept silent, careful to hear everything Henry Logan had to say.

Henry spoke loudly so the girls could hear: "Our woods are thicker than anything near where you live. Also, we begin the foothills to the mountains near here. In the spring, the creeks are full to overflowing and run very fast. You'll be crossing two creeks and you'll have to be careful not to lose your provisions when you cross. I'll show you how to get to the first creek and then I'll turn back. There's a trail on the other side to the second creek that you can't miss. Indians have been using the paths in these woods for hundreds of years."

Daniel asked, "How long till the first creek?"

Henry responded, "A few hours. You'll get there by midday, a good time to stop and give the mule a rest and let the horses drink. You could have something to eat as well, but don't waste too much time at your first stop. Try to get to where you see the second creek before you stop for the night. There are some flat places to camp but watch you don't get pushed into the water. The creeks are bursting now."

Bobby asked, "If the creeks are bursting, can we fish for our supper?"

Henry thought, then responded, "Yes, I suppose some fish over a fire would be better than the dried meats you're carrying. The fish likely are jumping out of the water—trout, striped bass if you're lucky. Did you bring fishing gear?"

Susan heard the question and shouted, "I have enough gear for three people and we could dig worms for bait!"

Beth laughed and said, "I'll be the lookout."

Henry glanced back at the girls. "A lookout is a good idea since there are four of you. The woods are hiding places for varmints of all kinds. You should set up a signal in case you sense something's wrong. Some varmints will pick on one, but four armed youngsters with rifles should be enough to scare the human variety away."

Beth asked, "What about animals?"

Henry said, "The animals have enough to eat now and won't bother you, especially if you make noise. You should strike up a song now and then. That should keep the deer away. Most animals will be tending to their young right now and the baby bears are out and around. You might see them up in the trees. Bears like to jump into the creeks to do their fishing. The babies climb on their mothers' backs. Takes baby bears awhile before they can fish by themselves. When you get near the creeks, watch out for snakes."

Beth asked, "What about Louise and Blackbeard? Do you think we'll see them?"

Henry laughed at that. "Not likely, but if she's there, Louise will see you first. Louise is used to people and enjoys entertaining youngsters. She can smell if you're happy or sad. Today, I think she'll keep to herself and look after her cub."

For the next three hours, they made their way through woods that seemed to get thicker, though a trail was always visible. The woods were alive with noises made by birds and small animals. Suddenly, they heard the rush of water and the trees seemed to thin out. Sunshine penetrated through the leaves.

Henry shouted, "All stay close together and follow me now." With that, he dismounted from his horse and turned a sharp left around a pile of small boulders. The boys followed him slowly single file, followed by the mule and the girls. They were still in deep forest but could hear the creek.

Henry pointed to a large oak tree that had three chop marks near its base. He said, "This is your sign post. When you get here, you turn right and go straight on." He pointed to a small path when he said, "This path will get you to a place at the first creek where you'll have no great trouble crossing. You shouldn't delay in crossing, as you want to get to the second creek before night fall."

Bobby asked, "Is the second creek easy to find and to cross? Should we look for a special place?"

Henry said, "You'll see some boulders after you cross the first creek. They'll be sitting in a pile—maybe five round rocks. They mark the beginning of a path to the second creek. The path goes along beside some wild rapids and you'll have to follow it to where the rapids end. When you get to the second stream, follow the path to the left until the stream becomes small and shallow and can be crossed easily. But you'll have to find the path on the other side to the Black Eagle. After you cross, look for another big oak tree with three chop marks, upstream and not far from the rapids. When you find the tree, make a sharp left until you find the path. Go slowly so you don't miss it. Look for signs of other travelers having been nearby. You'll see the Black Eagle when you get to the end of the path. It should take you about three hours, depending on how quickly the mule can go."

Henry mounted his horse and said to the boys, "You're brave and up to this. Don't take unnecessary chances and move slowly. Hang together and talk over everything. We'll be looking forward to hearing your news on your return. Your folks will be proud of you."

He went back to the girls and whispered quietly so the boys couldn't hear, "Keep an eye out, both of you, and figure out a signal in case something seems not right. Find something that will make a loud noise. Make sure you all hang together and don't be shy. If you see something, say so, and out loud."

Beth already had placed a frying pan tied to the side of her saddle. In her belt, she kept a small iron shovel that she knew made a loud clang when it struck the pan. She could easily bang on the pan as she sat on her small pony. Henry Logan had seen this and smiled at Susan and Beth.

Susan said, "Thank you for your help, Mr. Logan. We'll let the boys act like leaders since they're up front. We know we're all in this together and we'll do our part." Both girls waved to him as Henry turned to return home.

CHAPTER 19

DEEP WOODS

BOBBY DIDN'T KNOW how he felt when Henry Logan left. He was the oldest and tallest of the four teenagers and cousin to the family at the Black Eagle, but he wasn't a natural leader. He could ride and shoot a pistol but was more at home with reading and arithmetic. He had a great feel for distance and numbers and could use a compass, which he always kept with him. But Henry's directions depended on piles of rocks, chops in trees, and almost invisible trails. Bobby knew the trails wouldn't be easy to find. He asked Daniel, "How do you feel about this now?"

"Bobby, I'm glad you're the leader," he answered.

Bobby grumbled, "Then call me Bob from now on."

Susan heard that and shouted, "Bob the leader, strike up a song. Beth will accompany you on the frying pan."

The boys looked back as Beth hit the pan with her shovel. The clang was loud and clear and caused birds to scramble. They could also hear the scatter of small forest animals. Susan laughed and said, "We should have signals. Three bangs for really bad and load your pistol, two for in-between and let's get together, and one if we see something interesting."

Daniel shouted, "That's crazy. If there's a problem, we bring the guns, period. And you keep banging hard till we get together."

Beth banged out a version of "Yankee Doodle" and replied, "No need to argue. How about a song?" She stopped banging and started humming and soon all four were singing. They continued for half an hour. The woods gradually thinned and grew lighter and finally opened to a flat muddy bank at the first creek.

Bobby thought he should get everyone's opinion before continuing. He stopped and looked back at the girls and shouted, "How is King George doing? Will he pass this water without bucking and turning away?"

Beth moved up on her pony and took hold of King George's reins while Susan followed on her pony to join the boys. Susan said, "King George doesn't like excitement. He needs to know we're with him all the way, or he won't move at all."

Beth suggested, "I could hold his rein from my pony and be right beside him. I think he'd like that. But I don't think I should lead."

The creek was shallow and rocky. The white, foamy water moved quickly but was no more than a foot deep as far as they could guess.

Daniel thought and disagreed. He said, "The only way to be sure is to hold him all the way across. I could do that. I'll take off my boots, hold his rein from the front and guide him. Maybe Beth could go alongside us slowly, and Susan could follow."

Susan said to Daniel, "Have you put your hand in that water? It's cold. And the bottom is rocky and could cut your feet. You'll have to keep your boots on. Do you have other boots?"

Bobby said, "I have an extra pair of short boots. King George is carrying them. Maybe I should lead him across."

Daniel looked at Bobby. "A mule's not a horse, you know. You have to let him know who's the leader and make him follow you."

"I can do that as well as any of you. Susan should be in front with Prince. Beth and I will follow, bringing along King George, and you follow us, hanging on to my horse."

While they talked, they were surrounded by a vibrant animal

kingdom. Every few minutes, large fish leaped out of the creek. Wolves could be heard not far away and, straight ahead, they could see a black mother bear with a baby bear on her back. The mother had caught a leaping fish and was trying to wade to the other side of the creek while carrying the cub.

Bobby saw the bears and said, "We need to wait till she makes it across. We could follow her. Try to remember how she makes her way."

Susan sang out a loud musical laugh at the sight of the mother and baby bear.

Beth shouted, "Is that you, Louise? We have sweets for Blackbeard!" The girls struck up a children's song and Beth beat time on the frying pan. The bear seemed oblivious to their presence and concentrated on getting across the creek's rushing water.

Bobby jumped from his horse and walked back to King George, whistling. When he got to the mule, he took the mule's rein and said, "No excitement now. I'm taking you across with Beth."

They watched the bears and could see the mother bear get to the other side. Susan lifted Prince and held him as she began to make her way across. Beth waited a bit and slowly followed as Bobby held King George's reins and walked carefully into the creek. Daniel came behind on his horse while loosely holding the rein to Bobby's horse. The two horses, one behind the other, moved slowly and neighed.

Susan began to hum to Prince as she led the way, and after a few minutes was singing. The dog seemed excited and ready to prance, but the sound of the rushing water affected him. He seemed happy to be in Susan's arms. Her pony walked steadily from mud to rock to mud again. Beth followed and sang along with Susan as Bobby led the mule. Bobby, splashed from head to toe, held onto the rein and kept speaking to the mule. The mule, also wet from the splashing creek, brayed quietly but followed slowly. After twenty minutes, they got to the other shore where they let the horses drink water from the creek.

Susan looked at Bobby. "You need to get into dry clothes or you'll get sick."

Daniel, also quite wet, said, "Take off your wet things and lay them out to dry. We should do some fishing here. The fish are just jumping out of the water."

Beth looked at Bobby. He was the oldest and shyest of all of them, and obviously didn't want to undress with them all looking at him. She said, "My dad's leather outer jacket is in my pack on King George. My grandmother insisted I take it, just in case. I think this is what she meant by in case."

She offered the jacket to Bobby but he stripped down to his bare chest instead and took a fish net from Susan, saying to Beth, "Thanks, but it's warm now and my clothes should dry quick enough. If they don't, I'll appreciate the jacket." He then moved to the creek, skipping over a few stones still wearing his outer boots. He shouted, "We don't need bait here. We just have to see if we can net a few."

Daniel also removed his shirt and joined Bobby with a long seine that he was able to drape through the rushing water. The two boys stayed in the creek for about half an hour and came out with four large trout. Bobby was delighted but felt cold. Beth greeted him with a large cloth which she handed him to use as a towel.

"Have you seen any boulders?" he asked.

"No, we've been watching you and unloaded some supplies from King George. Have some dried meat for now."

The girls looked at the four large fish that had to be stored some way. They decided to keep them in the net which they tied to the mule. They found some dried meat to eat and the bag of honey biscuits, as all of them were hungry. Prince happily roamed up and down the shore after chewing on a piece of dried meat.

Susan looked around for boulders but could see none in a pile.

The shore was dotted with numerous rocks, but none of the four knew which direction to look. Susan finally moved back under a large tree that dominated the shore line. There she saw that someone had been there earlier, leaving heavy footprints and broken branches. She sat down under the tree and took out a honey biscuit. As she lifted it to her mouth, she could see a small black shadow behind the tree.

She called out, "Is someone there?" She put the honey biscuit on a pile of sticks and moved back toward the creek where Beth was watching. Prince started barking and raced into the wood.

In an instant, they saw a small black bear with the honey biscuit in his mouth next to his very large mother. Prince was looking up at the mother bear. Susan raced in and lifted Prince, who was shaking with fear.

The mother bear looked at Susan, turned and disappeared into the wood. The baby bear followed his mother. Where the mother bear had stood were five scattered round boulders and the beginnings of a path.

CHAPTER 20
TO THE BLACK EAGLE

THOUGH THEY WERE sure they'd found the path they were seeking, they could not adjust to the changes in the forest. Sunlight filtered through the leaves of the new growth on the giant oaks and maples, but the evergreen trees were very large and dark. At times when the path took a turn, they saw little of the path in front of them.

Not seeing much ahead of them or each other, they slowly stopped speaking. They wouldn't admit to feeling frightened, but all were more alert to sounds and smells. They heard more wails of wolves and loud, almost thunderous crashes of branches and brush being stepped on somewhere not far from them, but they could not be sure who or what made the loud sounds. The small forest animals—squirrels, raccoons and chipmunks—had found plenty of places to stash their nuts and take refuge from the larger animals and they weren't easily seen at all.

Bobby shouted back to the girls, "Time for a song or a story. The sounds will bounce off the trunks of these giant oaks."

Susan replied, "Yes, bounce back and we won't be able to hear the sounds of the varmints hiding."

Bobby and Daniel rode ahead, single file, followed by King

George. Behind them Susan followed on a pony, trailed by Prince. Beth stayed in the rear and held her frying pan with her shovel tucked into her belt.

Once the forest darkened, Prince began to growl. Susan looked down at him, asking aloud, "What do you smell? Is someone here?"

Beth looked at the young dog and said, "He thinks there are people around. He didn't sound like that when he saw Blackbeard, though the sight of Louise frightened him. He knows the smell of people and he's brave around them. He just jumped into the bed with all of us at the Logan's."

Susan wasn't sure, "Yes, but he knew us, and he's basically friendly. He's making unfriendly sounds now, and that's new for him." Susan shouted up to Bobby and Daniel, "Better be ready for something. Prince smells a rat, probably the human kind. Maybe one of you should get a gun ready?"

Daniel replied, "They're ready and we're holding them. The trouble is we won't be able to see much here in the woods. It's easy for any varmint to watch us, with King George and four ponies in a line. If anything happens, remember to come up quickly and form a circle. That will give us a little cover."

Bobby shouted, "Not much room for a circle here in the woods. Watch your backs and don't linger. It's best if we stay close together."

For several hours, they moved slowly in close proximity to each other. Prince growled most of the time. Twice he wandered into the close trees, barked loudly and quickly returned to Susan. At an especially dark spot on the trail, Susan lifted him into her lap and let him ride the pony with her.

When Susan lifted Prince, Beth started drumming on her frying pan with her knife handle, and shouted, "Can you hear the frying pan?"

Bobby laughed, "That doesn't sound like a distress call. You'll have to knock it louder."

As he said that, Prince leaped from Susan's lap, jumped to the side of the path and barked as loudly as he could. Beth grabbed her pistol when he did that and pounded on the frying pan, shouting, "How about that?"

Bobby turned his horse around and came back to the place where Prince still stood barking. He said, "Susan, go up ahead with Daniel, and take Prince with you. I'll stay back here with Beth. We'll all be safer that way. I've got my rifle loaded and ready, and Beth can free her hand to whack the frying pan."

Susan scooped up Prince and moved ahead of King George. When she reached him, she said to Daniel, "Do you think that maybe the smell of the fish is getting the forest animals excited?"

"No, those animals would rather eat us than dead fish. Let's try to move a little faster, to a place where we can at least see a little better." With that, he prodded his old horse, but the animal continued to move at its own slow pace.

Several hours later, they cleared the woods and came to a fast-moving stream. Narrower than the first and shallower, the water splashed high over the rocks that covered its bottom and moved rapidly. Remembering Henry Logan's instructions, they made a left turn and slowly continued down the waterside for another several hours. When the stream appeared to be narrow and relatively shallow, Daniel shouted, "Let's stop. This looks like a good place to cross."

By the time they stopped, the sun sat low in the sky and the stream lay in shadows. A chill breeze filled the air. They removed tents and cooking utensils from King George and let the mule and horses rest and drink from the stream.

The boys set up two small tents and placed blankets inside them. The girls arranged an iron grill and two iron pots to be used for cooking, and laid out the last of their provisions of dried meat and cider using metal plates and cups. The freshly caught fish from earlier that day were still tied up in the nets that caught them.

Taking advantage of the remaining daylight, Bobby and Daniel started a fire, while Susan removed the fish from the netting and cleaned them using a sharp hunting knife. She removed the heads and entrails, and scraped off some of the scales. Beth remained as the lookout through all their activity. She moved around the campsite slowly, keeping an eye to the edge of the wood while listening for unusual sounds.

Bobby and Daniel took the cleaned fish and rested them on the grill which sat on large sticks they'd balanced over the campfire. Susan held two small shovels she would use to turn the fish over, and to remove the fish once it looked that they were fully cooked.

Before the last fish was loaded over the fire, they could hear Beth scream and the loud banging of an iron shovel against the frying pan. Susan slid to the ground and hid behind the pile of cooking and camping equipment that had been loosely unloaded and strewn around the ground. She quickly loaded her pistol. Carrying their rifles, Bobby and Daniel separated, but took places behind the tents located between the campfire and the stream. They thought they couldn't be seen, but they could see the full campsite. They'd had their rifles loaded all day, and now tried aiming them without firing.

In a few minutes, they could see Beth being dragged toward the fire by a scruffy-looking bearded man, followed by an equally scruffy-looking bearded companion. The two thugs held pistols, wore rifles on their shoulders, and carried knives in their belts. Beth tried to pull away from her captor's grip and repeatedly screamed.

On hearing Beth's first scream, Bobby lifted his rifle and let off a shot. It missed high but caught the attention of the man dragging Beth. The man pulled out his pistol and shouted, "If you don't want this little lady to be hurt, come out now and drop your weapons. We have more arms than you and know how to use them. No use getting all of you killed on the same day." The second thug stayed two steps behind Beth.

Prince leaped from behind Susan and bit onto the pistol hand of the man holding Beth. The thug screamed in pain, but still held Beth around her neck. Prince tightened his grip on the thug's hand and refused to let go.

Bobby, Susan and Daniel could see a large, thunderous mass of an animal come up behind the second thug. The man smelled the beast and when he turned around, he leaped back in fright. Though fully armed, the thug chose not to use any of his weapons; instead, he immediately ran for the forest.

The gigantic black mother bear, moving quickly, soon towered over Beth and the man who'd captured her. Before Beth's captor had a chance to turn around and see her, the bear grunted mildly and promptly swatted the thug on the top of his head, causing him to fall and drop his pistol. Prince let go of the man's hand as they both fell, and Beth quickly crawled to safety, where she took hold of Prince and grabbed the pistol.

The bear came up beside Beth and moved toward the thug. He looked up, terrified, and finally stood and scurried into the forest. The top of his head bled profusely as did the outside of his right hand. He could barely see as the blood dripping down from his scalp filled his eyes.

The bear lingered for a moment and took a close look at Beth, Susan and the boys. She quickly turned around and headed into the forest. Susan breathed a loud sigh of relief, while Daniel started laughing nervously.

Bobby looked around, saying, "Too bad I'm such a poor shot," to which Susan replied, "Good thing, too. You probably would have gotten Beth or the bear."

Bobby then looked at Beth, saying, "Are you hurt? Do you think that was Louise? Is Blackbeard not far behind?"

Beth took a deep breath. Though she knew the danger was over, she was near tears. She didn't know what to say. "I suppose a bear or a rifle is better than a frying pan when things get rough. What a smell that man had! Would you all mind if I take a little swim and a wash in the creek before we eat?"

Nobody said anything until Susan came over to Beth and said, "What a great idea. I wanted to go in myself and I have some soap from the Logan's." She grabbed a small leather bag and pulled Beth's hand. Susan peered into her leather bag and handed the few remaining honey biscuits to Daniel.

She said to Beth, "Let's go to where the water is a little deeper." Then she pulled Beth along the edge of the stream to where they would be slightly hidden by some shrubs. Beth breathed deeply but didn't object.

Bobby and Daniel looked around for an obvious spot for the biscuits and found a small tree stump not far from the campfire. They left the biscuits on top of the stump and Daniel took the last raw fish and laid it on the ground beside the stump. He said, "We don't have much else to give them, but they've saved us today."

When the girls returned, the four took their guns and sat by the fire, paying no mind to the tree stump. They ate their fresh grilled fish, saw that the horses and ponies were comfortable and properly tied up to trees in the woods, and found a comfortable spot for King George. Dark had come when they realized they were all weary from the long trek and anxiety of the last two days.

The tents were ready. Without much delay all four decided to sleep. They didn't bother to discuss the need for a lookout, as all were too tired to think about it. Somehow the afternoon's events gave them a feeling of confidence. They didn't think the two thugs would return soon. They also hoped the bear wouldn't wander too far if she found a little food. Prince slept beside the girls' small tent, with his legs under the tent's covering. He didn't make a sound all night and neither did the girls or boys.

In the morning, the honey biscuits and the uncooked fish were gone, and the campsite showed signs of a visit from some large animals. Pots and camping equipment were thrown about. The ponies, horses and King George remained tied up roughly where they were the night before, but likely hadn't spent a restful night.

The four packed the camping gear and tents and started out across the stream. The water was shallow, not running too quickly, and easy to cross. On the other side, they could see scuff marks and footprints which they followed and soon found a tree with three chopped marks. Following Henry Logan's instructions, they took a sharp left and soon found the path. They made it to the Black Eagle by early afternoon.

CHAPTER 21

BURR MAKES HIS WAY

URR POWELL, HIS father's second son and father of ten himself, was used to planning the future. He spent most of his days sitting at a desk, drafting legislative proposals for introduction to the Virginia General Assembly. Often he designed proposals to assist wealthy individuals and companies doing business with the Commonwealth of Virginia. Sometimes these people claimed they were starting new businesses; sometimes they had secret designs. Burr never questioned their motivations. He did not intentionally seek payment for his services, but gifts came his way. He was careful to introduce his bills only for people with whom he'd become familiar. A committee chairman, he kept informed of new business ventures and over the years he'd been successful in amassing a relatively large fortune.

Burr was not an active person. He'd always been overweight and couldn't walk very far without a cane. He could not mount a horse, and now that he'd reached his forties, he simply waited while others did all the physical tasks required for his daily life. His wife, Anna, never complained, but she ran the household in a way that protected Burr. Anna saw to all household activities, supervised the education of the children, and acted as a pleasant hostess or guest at all the social events expected of the wife of a prominent member of the General Assembly.

Burr loved his children and badly wanted a son to take over his business interests and, if possible, his profession. He read with his boys and spoke with them often about Virginia, the General Assembly, the importance of elections, and the Powell family. He felt his family had played an essential role in creating the new nation and he wanted his children to be enthusiastic participants in building the country in the future. To Burr, that meant keeping business growing, attracting new people to the area, and amassing as much land as possible. This journey to see Billy was part of Burr's plan to involve his son John in the future and to keep Leven's warrants in the family.

Burr's son, John, at sixteen years of age, knew quite a lot about his father's profession, and he had no intention of pursuing it for himself. He'd often talked about the work of the assembly to friends and his siblings, especially Beth, his younger sister. John doubted his father's aims in this adventure to overtake his uncle Billy. He never argued with his father openly and wished that Beth had come along with him rather than staying back at the Logan's. John had often persuaded Beth to speak to his father when he didn't have the courage to do so himself. Beth was active, outgoing and John trusted her judgment completely. Naturally introspective, John disliked being pushed into things by his father.

John knew his father wanted to acquire something by this adventure, but he really didn't want to know too much about the details. He persuaded himself that he really didn't want to be involved at all. The idea of going on a hunting or fishing trip with his father was simply ludicrous.

They'd spent one day at the Logan farm and John had enjoyed sleeping in the barn with the Logan boys. Burr had conferred there with Henry Logan and agreed to take four long rifles for his adventure in meeting Billy. He'd also decided to leave Beth in the Logan's care as she seemed to enjoy the company of the Logan girls, Amy and Hannah. At least Beth gave him no arguments. He and John bade them all a quick farewell, with the promise to see them before too long. Henry promised to bring Beth back to her grandmother by the next day or so.

While Burr could handle a gun as could John, they were not trained in militia skills and neither were great shots. Burr knew about Walsh and knew that he could never have too many weapons for the possible encounters facing them.

They started off for the Black Eagle from the Logan farmhouse on a warm spring day. They rode in a small buggy pulled by a single horse. The buggy could give them some shelter from sun and rain and allowed some cover for their camping equipment and rifles. The horse, a tall, older steed, while not the fastest horse they could have chosen, was reliable and wouldn't frighten easily. The horse, named Charger, was black and sleepy in appearance.

Burr drove the buggy and John asked, "How did Charger get his name? He wouldn't charge anyone or anything if he wasn't driven into it."

Burr laughed, "But he's forced into everything he does. He has no choice. In the end, he's there and powerfully. If something needs charging, he'll do it, though I don't know who named him or why. I think General Washington had a Charger and people everywhere named their animals and children for Washington whenever they could. Everyone wants to have a piece of the hero."

John shrugged and looked out onto the main road to Winchester. It was a stony thoroughfare, just wide enough to allow two buggies like theirs to pass each other when going in opposite directions. The sides of the roads were dirt and brush from which could be seen the beginnings of lovely mountain wildflowers, mostly in light blue and pink.

John asked his father, who was beginning to wheeze and breathe heavily, "Are you well, Father? Do you want me to drive Charger? You could lie down and rest a bit in the back. There is only one direction for us to go to the Black Eagle."

"No, I'll drive a bit longer. The spring air gets to my throat. I suppose I should get out more. It would help my breathing. I am not ill. How are you taking this?"

"Father, could you explain your reason for doing this? You really don't want to hunt or fish and the woods have always frightened you. Why take me? I'm no hunter or fisherman, and I could live without camping in the woods. You should have taken Beth."

"It's only one night of camping. We'll be at the Black Eagle tomorrow and there are some lovely streams. We could catch some fish for supper. What do you think? We could stop by mid-afternoon to get there by early tomorrow."

John, a tall, thin boy with a narrow waist and hollow shoulders, shivered. He reached for the leather jacket his mother had given him at the last moment before they'd left their home to visit his grandmother. At the time, his mother had said, "Be careful. Don't take chances and look to your own safety." She always said things like that, so he'd simply smiled and waved his goodbye while taking the jacket.

"That would be fine. But why are we doing this, Father?" John put on the jacket and soon felt hot in the spring sunshine.

"Your Uncle Billy will need all the help he can get, and it's time for you to see how the world works and what your place might be in it."

"Does that take a gunfight? Shouldn't this be a job for the militia? You could have called troops out. They can shoot straight at least. Why do you think I could help in this kind of event?"

"But this is a Powell event, not a General Assembly of Virginia event. Billy has your grandfather's warrants for land in Ohio and thugs are trying to take the property away from him. The warrants are for Powell land and you are a Powell. You should be excited to be included in this. It could mean something for your future. You're sixteen and need to think of who you'll be and how you will live."

"Father, you didn't raise me to be a farmer or a pioneer. That's Beth you are thinking about, and you decided not to take her."

"Beth's only fourteen and your mother has great plans for her future, whether she knows it or not. Young women have to marry to count for something in society, and Mother has already chosen a few likely brothers-in-law for you."

"Beth will have nothing to do with it. You'll see. She cares nothing for a place in society. She loves the outdoors, the woods, the animals, and she's strong and brave. You'll have trouble persuading her to look to the higher reaches of society."

Burr laughed. "You'd be surprised how a big party and gifts can change a girl's opinion. She hasn't yet had attentions paid to her. She'll love it. And what about you? Have you thought of paying suit to a young woman? You'll need to grow up a bit and have a fortune or a living to do that. You have to offer a young woman a decent future if you want to settle and have a family. Have you thought that through?"

John didn't expect this kind of conversation. He said, "Father, I have thought of my future, but not in the way you expect. I don't care to settle down. I want to see our country, yes, but I first want to see part of the world. I want to study and learn. I thought to join the navy. I think I'd like to visit some of the great ports."

Burr couldn't believe his ears. "The navy? Where did you get an idea like that? Have you ever seen a great ship? Do you know what it's like to work on one of those? Do you know anything about the people who serve on navy ships? I think you should think some more. There are other ways to learn and see the world."

John didn't answer. They drove several hours and stopped by

a shady spot at the side of the road. They unhitched Charger and let him rest and chew on the spring grass while they drank and ate from the provisions they'd brought with them, some sliced ham and homemade beer.

When they started out again, Burr continued the conversation. He said, "Have you thought of attending a university? There's the College of New Jersey where Billy attended. Ben Franklin started a university in Philadelphia awhile back, and we still have William and Mary. Those are places you could learn about many things. Washington got his surveyor's license from William and Mary."

John said nothing, as he felt like he was being cornered into some decision he wanted to consider without being pushed. He said, "Maybe when we see him, I'll talk to Billy. It isn't something I've considered, but I do enjoy reading about the new uses of steam power. I'm fascinated by Fulton's steamboat."

Burr knew his son wasn't interested in talking, but he kept on. "Have you thought about what you'll do next year? Would you like a job in the assembly? I could find a committee that deals with commerce and navigation and the introduction of steamboats. You could meet the people who build them."

"Father, what would I do in the assembly? I would be a messenger, doing nothing of substance."

"You'd be learning about things in a practical way, from people who know their business. You'd also be meeting people. You could be learning some social skills, so you can present yourself in an appropriate way to other people."

John smirked. "You mean, take a place in society? I thought Washington led a revolution against monarchy and aristocracy. Now you want to rebuild those social divisions again?" John remembered the conversation at his grandmother's only a few days earlier. While he didn't say so at the time, he'd been impressed with his grandfather's letters. He and Beth had looked over several and that brought back old memories of Leven, their grandfather, and long talks they'd had with him.

Burr could hear John's anxiety and apprehension about his future. He said, "The future doesn't just happen. You have to make it happen. Every country has a social order, whether you like it or not. If you want to get ahead in life, you must learn to deal with people. There will always be someone ahead of you or with something you want. You have to learn to be persuasive, to know who you are and present yourself to others in a positive way. Washington knew that. He even wrote a little book about proper manners and how to behave in society."

"That's not what I'm talking about. It's the business of some people taking all the wealth and bankrupting everyone else. Washington was against that. He thought government should serve the people, not just the politicians. He didn't like politics and looked to the west for the country's growth. He wanted us to build up ourselves, and not get involved in foreign entanglements. I think he was right. Politics in the old part of the country is about climbing over everyone else if you can get away with it."

Burr, trying to hold back anger, responded, "Politics is superior to warfare. At least the assembly discusses issues. Men like Walsh let their guns do the talking, and that's why we're on the way to find Billy. No political system can tolerate too many people who want to take over by violence, without discussion or debate. That goes for foreign powers and our own homegrown thugs."

John continued, "Did you ever think of going west, Father? That was where Grandfather's heart was, same as Washington. What about you?"

"Someone has to do the dirty work of keeping things together at home. Your grandmother kept us all alive during the revolution, while your grandfather was away with the military. Now Cuthbert and I do the same for the family. We see to it that peace is observed and people have food on the table. It isn't heroic or solitary work. You may think that's not building the country, but it is. We create a place where people can come, start new farms and businesses, and support their families. That's growth, too. We deal with all kinds of people and we respect their views in elections. We do what we think is best for all of us."

John didn't accept the argument. He said, "I want a different future than that. I want to work for myself while building up the country. I think Washington saw the whole country, or what it could be. It takes courage to build the new. I think I want to talk to Uncle Billy."

They didn't stop to fish, but ate some more of the ham and beer that night. They arrived at the Black Eagle the next day by late afternoon.

CHAPTER 22

BILLY POWELL

BILLY POWELL, A powerful man of forty, knew a great deal about close scrapes and violent confrontations. He'd started and finished them, from time to time, all his life. Quick on his feet and quite tall, he'd sometimes been able to impress people and talk his way out of difficulties. Sometimes he simply vanished before things got too rough. But when principles were at stake, he always stood his ground. He always defended what was his, even against difficult odds.

He knew how to defend himself because he often had to do that. He could wrestle, wield a knife and shoot a pistol as well as any man. More than once he'd fought off three and four attackers, sometimes by himself with no assistance from anyone. He wasn't used to asking for help from others.

Billy sat by a campfire in the woods on the outskirts of Winchester, waiting for George Morgan White Eyes, who was bringing a party of fighters. The group he expected would be a mixture of Indians loyal to George and children of veterans of the revolution, like him. He knew all of them from his years of settlement along the Ohio. He hoped the Ohio group had sufficient weapons.

Billy often did things on his own and willingly paid the price for it. Never married, he'd come close three times, but each time he'd either picked a fight with a prospective bride's father or ran up his debts too far to safely stay in one place for too long. He'd run away from women of whom his family had high opinions. Billy thought about the last broken engagement to a sweet eighteen-year-old with dark black hair and clear blue eyes, just five years earlier.

Billy shrugged with sadness at the memory. He thought that he wasn't a bad catch for a young girl of good family. He still had his looks. He had broad shoulders, light brown hair, and a finely shaved moustache. His father was a close friend of Washington. He had hopes for a decent future with his various investments and schemes.

Billy loved the girl, but thugs were out to get him. He couldn't endanger her or her family, or his family for that matter. He told himself that he likely would have made a poor husband. He'd never made many friends, mainly because he was always plotting his next project and he wasn't used to sharing his plans with anyone.

His father had changed all that. His father's warrants presented a different project, one he'd never planned for. They entitled the bearer, Billy, to thousands of acres along the Ohio River, and his father had told him that they were for him alone, if he could use them to build up the country.

Leven had invoked the family's shared memory of Washington. With tears in his eyes, he'd said, "Billy, this is what we all fought for—for a chance to make a living and build a new country. We should be building new towns, new businesses, and making the place safe for people and families who will come. So many died following Washington. He'd have wanted you to have these warrants; he remembered you. He knew you wanted to explore and move ahead, not be caught up in politics and pleasing people."

What could he have said to his old father? They both remembered Washington and Billy felt overwhelmed by the gift. He also knew his brother Burr had an eye on the warrants. If he hadn't accepted them, the land would've been Burr's.

Billy reminisced about the old days and his brothers. They'd spent their childhood years often fighting with each other, but he couldn't remember why they fought. Burr and Cuthbert were always getting someone to back them up, always screaming for help if they couldn't handle fights on their own. He'd come to their rescue more than once.

He laughed thinking about Cuthbert following him into a rushing creek and losing his balance. Cuthbert must have been about six and was very much attached to Jane, then about ten years old. Cuthbert believed everything Billy said and looked up to him, though Billy was only twelve. Billy was a hero to Cuthbert, even though Billy sometimes teased him and played tricks on him.

That spring day, Billy remembered, he'd waded into a creek and sat down on a rock, yelling to Cuthbert, "Come in; I'm in trouble."

Cuthbert, who'd been holding Jane's hand at the water's edge, jumped into the cold, rushing water yelling, "I'm coming!" Soon Cuthbert fell and hit his head on a rock. Luckily, Jane was nearby and quickly lifted her little brother, all the while shouting at Billy. Burr stood on the shore watching. Billy remembered that Burr, age nine, never moved and never got himself wet that day. Just like the politician he turned out to be.

Billy knew that Jane would be surprised to know that George Morgan White Eyes still lived. George had changed so much over the last five years. Jane would remember a young, thin college man, quick to speak his mind and to uphold the beliefs of his vice president, Aaron Burr. Now, after years building a home in the Ohio wilderness, he had the scars of a fighter and man of action. Jane remembered a boy. This new George was an Indian chief like his father. Billy wondered what Jane would think about a future with George. He imagined that Cuthbert gave her warnings, but Mother?

Mother always looked to the west and likely would want Jane to do the same.

Billy shrugged, knowing he couldn't predict his sister's behavior. Who said women were simple? Jane had run her mother's house, cared for the elderly women now living there, taught school, and kept a fine vegetable garden after helping to raise the ten Powell children. There was nothing soft or easy about Jane. That's one of the reasons George was coming back, to persuade Jane to join him. He needed her strength and intelligence in the new world he was building.

CHAPTER 23

GEORGE MORGAN WHITE EYES

G EORGE MORGAN WHITE Eyes left his Lenape village accompanied by eight men. Three were cousins who had families, but he'd persuaded them to come with him. They all knew Billy and were well-trained fighters. They could shoot rifles and arrows, throw knives, and understand military strategy. They'd also fought off numerous raids on the village from various bands of thugs and Shawnee intruders. In their absence, George had appointed twenty men to see to village security.

The other five of George's men were children of revolutionary war veterans whose families had settled along the Ohio. They lived as part of the Lenape nation but were patriotic Americans; younger men who hadn't yet taken wives. With talk of a new war with England in the air, they were as ready to fight as their fathers had. To them, this business for Billy was a small example of fighting for justice. They saw Billy as a rightful son of the revolution. Those trying to seize his property were the undeserving faceless rich trying to take property from the honest and deserving.

In addition, George's operation presented an opportunity to visit the East where the five young frontiersmen had family. Two of them planned to visit Baltimore, where one had some cousins and the other a living grandmother. The other three looked forward to visits to towns between Richmond and Norfolk. All expected to be introduced to relatives they'd never met and the prospect made them nervous.

The five young men carried letters and gifts for relatives prepared by their parents. Before leaving Ohio, George said to them, "You'll be meeting some ladies, selected for you by family. I hope that goes well. In any case, I and your parents expect you back in Ohio. If you marry, your wives will be welcome. We'll plan a special Lenape wedding for all who want it on your return."

George knew that his five young fighters looked forward to a skirmish in the woods that he hoped to avoid. By having a large and well-armed party, he hoped that Walsh would simply disappear and leave Billy to take his property peacefully.

George and Billy had been close friends for many years. George also was chief of his village and its chief negotiator. He was a newly elected representative in the Ohio House of Representatives. If all went well in Virginia, Billy's land would be added to his, which would increase the population of Adams County, settled by many revolutionary war veterans and named for Vice President Adams. George thought that in time, with planning and peace, he might run for election as a new member of the United States Congress. If his county had the land and offered opportunity, he believed its population would grow. He was willing to work hard to make it grow.

George's men were well aware of the politics of the day. Jefferson had purchased an enormous tract of land west of the Mississippi from Napoleon, some said illegally. Where did Jefferson get the money to pay for it? There was virtually no money anywhere in the country. Many people thought Jefferson's love for the French made him pursue the Louisiana Purchase. Other people said it was Napoleon's love of Washington that motivated the French to sell at a reasonable price. Nobody really knew the amount of land involved. It stretched from the Mississippi River to the Rockies and went from Mexico and Louisiana into western Canada. Napoleon certainly wanted the land out of the hands of the English.

The British were seizing American ships and acting as if they owned the newly independent states. Most people were tired of war and there was division among the Indian tribes in Ohio. Chief Tecumseh in the north had always favored the English. If a new war came, he'd likely side with the English and their Canadian allies. George's father and his people always had sided with Washington and favored independence. George wanted his new state of Ohio to be a strong, independent partner in the new union of states.

George thought about the task ahead and his own personal future. He loved Billy like a brother as they had been through much together. During the revolution, George's father had developed a friendship with Leven Powell, Billy's father. Both Billy and George were present at several meetings where Washington, Leven, Chief White Eyes and some military commanders discussed the Lenape participation in the war in the west.

George remembered telling Jane about these meetings. At the time, she had teased him, saying he looked more like Washington than his own father. George was over six foot three, with a swarthy skin color and crystal blue eyes. He inherited his height and skin from his Lenape father, his blue eyes from his English mother. His prominent nose came from someplace unknown, but that was the feature that Jane said made him look like Washington. Now that he was fully grown and his shoulders had widened to the build of a man who did work on horseback, he really was about the size of Washington.

George sighed, remembering how he had learned of the murder

of his parents at the hands of an army scout. He remembered how shocked Leven and Mrs. Powell were at the time and how they'd taken him into their home until Congress voted him a scholarship to the College of New Jersey. They were only teenagers at the time, but he and Jane had formed a serious friendship then. He kept in touch with her through Cuthbert for several years until he went to work for vice president Aaron Burr. He thought Leven and Mrs. Powell would not have objected if he had announced his wish to court Jane.

But history intervened. Burr killed Hamilton in a duel, giving Jefferson the opportunity to remove Burr from the ticket as vice president in 1804. Now someone in power wanted George and his family dead. George had always thought agents of Jefferson had killed his parents. He couldn't endanger Jane and her family. Under the circumstances, George had postponed thoughts of marriage to Jane and agreed to accompany Burr on a trip to look over the new western lands. At the time, George had hoped he could soon return. Once again, that didn't happen.

When the Burr party got to Ohio, George decided to stay with the Lenape village while Burr and the rest of the party went south. Several days later, the village was attacked by a band of American army scouts. George's Lenape cousins protected him from the raid that clearly was intended to kill Burr. While Burr had left Ohio, George ended up fighting in a rather large skirmish which left nine Lenape dead. George owed a great debt to his Lenape cousins. After the fight, commanded by the old Lenape chief, he married a Lenape girl and a year later she died giving him a son.

George named the little boy George, after Washington, and from the day he was born, the baby was large boned, blue-eyed, and very bright. Little George was now three years old and staying with his maternal grandmother back at the Lenape village. When the old chief died last year, George Morgan White Eyes became chief, presiding over a village of about three hundred, including the families of many revolutionary war veterans.

When George heard from Billy through a messenger that Walsh had physically threatened him and demanded his land warrants, George became concerned. He knew that Walsh worked for a large land corporation and probably had cheated and killed before. George thought that Walsh was somehow an agent of Jefferson, and while Jefferson was no longer president, he still had considerable prestige and power.

George, like Aaron Burr, had developed a strong dislike for Jefferson and everything associated with him. He thought Jefferson could write; the Declaration of Independence was evidence of that. But Jefferson had not participated in the actual creation of the government, the Constitution, and the idea of a union of states replacing the awkward Articles of Confederation. Jefferson had never considered the difficulties facing freely elected officials sharing power. Jefferson had never worn a uniform and fought for the country. During the revolution, Jefferson had lived in France, a monarchy, surrounded by aristocrats who treated him very well.

Jefferson had learned a great deal about politics in France, George thought. Since George blamed Jefferson for the murder of his parents, he had decided that Jefferson didn't care who he killed if it accomplished a means to his end. A few dark-skinned victims meant nothing to a man who insisted on keeping slaves in a revolutionary period when many Virginia planters had freed theirs. Jefferson thought himself an aristocrat, though he was good at writing idealistic republican prose. He kept slaves because he thought it was proper for an aristocrat to own other people.

How different from Burr! Burr thought anyone with a soul should be heard. He thought women had souls and should be allowed to vote. He thought that anyone who labored in the real world to support self and family should also be allowed to vote. Jefferson was terrified of Burr and the votes of women and big cities that Burr's ideas represented. Jefferson, seeing himself the landed aristocrat, despised cities and the people living in them.

George agreed with Burr and this brought back thoughts of Jane. He needed her now and this time he planned to ask. Sadly, Leven was no longer alive, but he could ask Mrs. Powell who he knew would certainly support him. He hoped he could persuade Jane to share his life in the west.

George had sent a messenger ahead to the Black Eagle to see if anyone knew anything about the whereabouts of Walsh. The messenger had left the village two days ahead of George and his party.

George and his eight men came fully armed in a procession of six men on horseback and two men driving a mule-drawn wagon full of arms and ammunition. George knew where to find Billy at an appointed campsite near Winchester. They would await the messenger who had detailed instructions about where to find them.

CHAPTER 24

THE BLACK EAGLE

On horseback, Bobby and Daniel led King George, who carried their gear. They were followed by Susan and Beth, also on horseback. Prince, the dog, sensing they finally were coming to a destination, decided to lead the whole party, barking happily and wagging his tail in front of the procession.

Leaving the woods, they arrived at the Black Eagle from the rear and could see smoke coming from the kitchen structure behind and adjacent to the tavern. They could also see, about a hundred yards back of the kitchen, a small, white two-story house.

Bobby said to Daniel, "That's Henry Silver's house back of the tavern where his family lives. I've been there a few times with my parents. Should we stop there?"

"You're supposed to see Henry Silver. He'll be at the Black Eagle."

"But we're bringing a ham. That's for his family. Maybe we would be a bother to him at the tavern?"

Beth rode up and after hearing the conversation, she said, "Let's go to the house. We're here to get information, and Mrs. Silver probably will know as much as Henry. I know she and your grandmother send each other messages and things all the time. Amy Logan told me about it."

Prince, listening to the conversation, looked up at Beth. He then turned around and took off as fast as he could and ran directly to the house. Susan followed him on her pony but could barely keep up. When the dog got to the house, he barked as he stopped before steps that led up to the small front porch. He barked as loudly as he could until Anna Silver opened the front door.

Anna was a tall, thin woman of fifty. She had her graying hair pulled back and wore a multicolored hand-woven jacket. She took a few steps onto the porch, looked down at the dog and said, "My goodness. What's a little fellow like you doing here in the wild woods?"

Susan came up behind him, saying, "Excuse us, ma'am. I'm Susan Carpenter. My brother and I are here with Bobby Potter and Beth Powell. Our grandmothers sent us to find out what you might know about Billy Powell."

Anna looked at Susan and smiled. While Susan spoke, Anna could see Bobby, Daniel and Beth approaching.

Bobby and Daniel dismounted their horses and went back to the mule where they found the ham. When they returned to the front porch, Bobby stood as erectly as he could and said, "Miss Anna, we're bringing you greetings from my grandmother Dorothy. She's sent you a ham and a letter for Henry Silver."

Bobby and Daniel carried the large ham up the front steps, laid it down near the front door, and Bobby pulled the letter out of a back pocket and handed it to Anna. She placed it in an inside pocket of her jacket and then grabbed Bobby and kissed him, saying, "You've grown a foot since I saw you last. Let me look at you. I think you're like your daddy."

Bobby felt embarrassed but smiled at Anna. With her arm on his shoulder, she said, "Thank you. It's always a pleasure to hear from Dorothy." Looking at Beth and Susan, she continued, "Dorothy and Henry are first cousins and we love to hear from her. Please bring your horses to the back of the house and then come in for some refreshment. You must be tired from your journey. Henry will be back here in about an hour and you can speak to him then."

Anna opened the front door and motioned to someone in the house. Soon a tall, dark young man with shoulder-length black hair but no beard emerged. She said to the four visitors, "This is my grandson Dave. He'll take care of the young ladies' ponies. Susan and Beth, please come in and make yourselves comfortable. You can wash up in the back and you're welcome to join us for our afternoon meal."

Beth replied, "Thank you, Mrs. Silver. I'm here because I expect my father and brother to arrive here. They took the main road and should be at the Black Eagle today. Billy is my uncle and we all worry about him."

"No need to worry now. Wait till Henry comes and then you can tell us everything. Go inside and have a little rest."

Susan said, "We saw some varmints in the woods. One pulled a gun and held Beth against her will."

Anna looked concerned and moved toward Beth, putting her arm on Beth's shoulder. "Well, you look like you've survived. I suppose the four of you were too much for the lowly varmint."

Susan burst out, "Yes, the four of us and a great mother bear. She swatted the varmint from behind and he ran away."

Anna laughed. "A bear? And she didn't harm any of you? We have Marcus the Magician with us now. He knows all about bears as he had one as part of his entertainment and lost her last year. When Dave comes back, I'll tell him to go up to the tavern and tell Henry to bring Marcus back here to share our refreshments. I'm sure we'd all love to hear about the bear and Marcus might have something to say about it."

An hour later, Henry Silver entered the house, accompanied by Marcus the Magician. Henry had grey hair tied back behind his head, and stood tall with broad shoulders. He was slim, almost gaunt, and stooped slightly. He was clean shaven, and his eyes seem to droop as if he were sleepy. Marcus was short, with very broad shoulders, wild and curly black hair, a well-trimmed beard, and a quick, energetic dancing step.

When Henry opened the front door, Prince began to bark and Dave quickly took the young dog to the rear of the house. Anna reached into her jacket and gave Henry Dorothy's letter, which he opened immediately and read. Marcus bowed to Anna and the house full of teenagers. He said, "I'm honored to be invited here. Can I repay you this afternoon with a small entertainment, just for the family?"

Anna replied, "Please sit down and make yourself comfortable. We have some roast beef and potatoes and a little beer besides. These four visitors have a story to tell us and you may be interested that it includes a bear."

Marcus laughed out loud when he heard this. "I think you've met my Louise. She loves young people. When did you see her last?"

Susan replied, "Just yesterday." Susan and Beth then told the whole story of leaving the Logan farm, traveling through the woods, seeing the bear, and escaping danger from the two human thugs with the bear's help.

Marcus thought out loud, "Do you think she followed you here? She followed you all the way from the Logan place?" He then turned to Henry, adding, "I would much appreciate an opportunity to do a real entertainment. I have my guitar and apparatus for magic and bear tricks. If Louise is near, maybe she'll come back to me."

Beth replied, "It's not just Louise. She has a cub we call Blackbeard and we've been feeding him honey biscuits all the way since the Logan's. Louise swam across one of the streams with him on her back."

Marcus smiled, "What a lovely girl she is. I'm afraid I have no honey biscuits, but I do know what Louise likes and have a sack of that back at the Black Eagle."

Henry replied, "I'll look forward to it. Perhaps behind the kitchen? There's more space there than in the front, and we can let everyone nearby know about it. We have a big drum to bang on to get people to gather."

Marcus leaped up. "I will get ready. Perhaps in two hours?" He immediately stood, thanked Anna profusely, and left for the tavern. Anna put some beef and potatoes on a plate for him to take with him, saying, "Get something to drink at the tavern."

When Marcus left, Henry stood and insisted that everyone listen to Dorothy's letter. He read, "We are concerned about Billy Powell who is somewhere near Winchester. If you've heard anything, please send word with these grandchildren and send them back as soon as you can by the main road."

Henry looked at Bobby and said, "Today I have nothing to tell you, but I know there are people here now who are waiting to see and hear from someone. Could you wait a day? It's safest if you all leave during the morning to take advantage of the light. Wait for Marcus and his entertainment. You'll enjoy that and somebody may show up that we can recognize. Beth needs to wait for her father and brother anyway."

The four teenagers looked at each other but said nothing. Bobby finally turned to Henry and said, "We need to have something to tell the grandmothers. We'll stay, if it's no trouble to you."

Anna looked at her grandson, who immediately looked at the ceiling. For that night, the two boys would share Dave's bed. The girls happily agreed to move into a bedroom that once had been home to the Silvers' three daughters. The daughters were now married and living on nearby farms of their own. Beth and Susan insisted that Prince stay with them.

After the teenagers had eaten, they found their rooms for the evening and unpacked their few things. Henry left for the tavern and an hour later the sounds of a large bass drum rang through the valley. The kitchen chimney smoked and neighbors from nearby farms soon began to appear at the front of the Black Eagle. Several guests of the inn also began to move to the rear where Marcus had prepared his apparatus: a small stage held a bench for him to sit or stand on, two four-step ladders topped by wide platforms each large enough to hold a bear, and a table supported closed containers good for magic tricks and treats as needed. Marcus carried a guitar attached to an elaborate belt around his neck.

The Black Eagle sat back from the main road. A two-story building, it held a large barroom on the main level and a large sleeping room on the second floor. The barroom held a few tables where guests and visitors could order food and drink. Inside, a tall frontiersman sat at a table with a beer, next to the tavern's lone window. In the front, a large wraparound porch held wooden furniture arranged at random. On the porch, two men sipped beers at a table and looked down the path that led from the main road to the tavern. They ignored the drum announcement. One man's head and right hand were wrapped in bandages.

CHAPTER 25

THE SHOW

WHEN THEY HEARD the drum from the rear of the Black Eagle, most inn guests and neighbors from nearby farms dropped what they were doing and prepared for a welcome break in their day. They expected some local announcements or a short entertainment and a chance to see neighbors. Marcus' audience would include some elderly grandparents, a handful of children under the age of ten, and a variety of adults happy to get away from the chores of the day. The crowd numbered about fifty and included very few adult women. Most of the men came unarmed, though a few carried knives.

Burr Powell and his son John arrived at the Black Eagle just as the crowd began to gather. After tying up their cart at a railing, they entered the Black Eagle from the front door and found one lone frontiersman sitting at a table and looking out the window. Henry Silver was bent over whispering to him while everyone else had gone out for the entertainment.

When Burr entered the tavern, Henry turned to him and said, "Welcome to the Black Eagle. We're having a magic show out back. How can I help you?"

Burr removed his hat and bowed in a formal manner, saying, "I am Burr Powell of the Virginia General Assembly, and this is my son John. We are in these parts to hunt, fish and find my brother Billy, if you know anything about him."

The frontiersman stood and came over to Burr. He leaned to him and whispered, "Not so loud, sir. There are many people seeking your brother. I'm with a party here from Ohio to help him, if he should need that kind of help."

Burr looked at the frontiersman and said, "Do you know where I can find Billy? I'd like to talk to him and see if I can help in some way."

Henry spoke, "Welcome, sir. We've been expecting you. We have your daughter Beth with us and she's decided to help with the entertainment. Why don't you wash up outside, have a beer, and join us? We'll have much to talk about once our magician completes his show."

As he spoke, he could see that four other men had arrived and were conversing with the two men who'd been sitting on the front porch all morning. Henry nodded to the frontiersman, who in turn returned to the window table and sat down. He could see the six men on the porch clearly. They seemed to be having a heated exchange of opinions, but he couldn't clearly hear what they were saying.

Using the back door to the kitchen area, Burr and John left the barroom and washed up at a barrel. They then made their way to the improvised stage that now held Marcus the Magician and two four-step ladders with wide platforms fixed to the tops. Young girls stood next to both ladders, each wearing a red, white and blue sash. On the left, Susan Carpenter held a handful of sweet red candies; on the right stood Beth Powell, holding some sweet honey candies.

The standing crowd gathered near the stage and waited for Marcus to begin. He soon leaped up, did a short dance, bowed to the crowd, and began strumming his guitar. He sang two happy country tunes and then announced:

"Ladies and gentlemen, thank you for coming. My name is Marcus the Magician and I'm here to entertain you. I'll begin with a few demonstrations." Marcus looked at Dave, Henry's grandson, who leaped up onto the stage next to Marcus, carrying some papers and cards.

Marcus said to the crowd, "Dave knows his cards. Here, Dave, pick a card." Marcus held up the deck of cards and Dave selected one. For the next fifteen minutes, Marcus astounded the crowd by guessing the card, its location, and making cards pop out of the deck. He took young volunteers out of the audience, mostly young children of less than ten, and all of them received candies for their participation.

After the cards, Marcus bowed and pulled a small brass trumpet out of his vest. He asked the crowd facing the center of the stage to separate so that an aisle of about five feet divided the group in two. Marcus then blew a short, boisterous trumpet melody of four notes, which he repeated three times. When he finished, he took a deep breath and looked around.

Marcus heard a distant pounding and said to the crowd, "Please stay and don't be frightened." He then blew the four notes again, repeating them three times. The pounding grew louder and everyone heard it. Within ten minutes, the crowd could see a large black bear and a small bear cub approaching from the direction of the Silvers' house. The crowd watched as the bears came near, the cub following his mother, both seeming to tumble with joy. Soon the two bears were on the stage beside Marcus.

Marcus leaped for joy, shouting, "My Louise is back, and she's brought her baby cub!" Louise immediately climbed the ladder next to Susan, who gave her three candy treats. Blackbeard looked at his mother but did nothing. Beth moved toward him and gave him a small number of honey candies, which he gulped down instantly.

Everyone became transfixed with Louise, who stood on one leg on the platform affixed to the left ladder. Marcus started to sing as he strummed his guitar. Louise slowly lifted one foot after another while Marcus increased the speed of his song. Soon Louise appeared to dance. The crowd loved the whole performance, and soon shouted their approval. "Hooray for Marcus!! Cheers for Louise!!"

Marcus tied a red ribbon around Louise's neck. He didn't go near Blackbeard, but led Louise by the end of the ribbon to where her cub stood. Marcus turned to Louise and asked, "Have you come home?" The bear and her cub followed him to his cart tied to a tree near the rear of the tavern.

While this was happening, five men entered the front of the Black Eagle. The man whose head and hand had been bandaged had climbed on his horse and ridden away. The lone frontiersman left soon after, following him.

Henry remained at the bar and greeted the visitors. "Welcome to the Black Eagle. I'm sorry you've just missed our magic show. How can I help you?"

The leader of the group, a red-headed man with a black beard, said, "We're meeting up with some friends to go to Winchester. Can you recommend some places to stay or camp? Where would you suggest a large party of fifteen or twenty should camp?"

"Well, are you fishing? Hunting? What do you have in mind?"

The red-headed man said, "Call me Jack. We'll be hunting. I'm looking for Billy Powell and his party. Can you tell me if he's been to these parts?"

"No, but his brother, niece and nephew are here. Would you like to speak with them?"

"That might be a good idea. Where can I find them?"

"Just out back. Wait here and I'll get them."

CHAPTER 26
POLITICS AGAIN

A S THE CROWD broke up, Henry saw John Powell near the stage, talking to his sister, while Burr remained in the rear, talking to three of Henry's neighbors. Burr seemed to be enjoying himself. Henry made his way to the group and said to Burr, "Mr. Powell, there is a man out in the bar who has asked to speak with you. He says his name is Jack and he wants to find your brother Billy."

Burr thought a moment and asked, "What did you tell him? Do you know him?"

Henry looked down at his feet and then at his neighbors. "He's a rough sort and boasts of having a gang of fifteen or twenty. You and your boy John will be of little use against a crowd like that. Would you like to speak with him?"

Burr replied, "What else is a politician good for? Of course I'll talk to him." Burr put on his hat, straightened his shoulders and started walking toward the tavern.

Henry addressed his neighbors next. "Can you spare some time and bring some guns? We might spend an interesting day in the woods. If you are militia, bring your badges. I'll meet you at my house in an hour or so." Henry turned and quickly went back to the tavern, where he found Burr with a beer in one hand and his other arm on red-headed Jack's shoulder. He was expounding on the work of the General Assembly and the recent growth of western Virginia. At a distance, they looked as though they had struck up a friendship.

Henry heard Burr say, "We all want to grow and Virginia is becoming a really great state. It takes more than just land to grow. We need people and investment. People have to be there to make the land worth having. They have to settle farms, build towns, exercise their skills, and learn to trade. Without that, you might as well have a desert."

Jack replied, "Yes, but the lion's share of the wealth goes to the landowner. The owner decides what happens to the land. If you own it, you can build if you want. You could also sell it."

"Property is more complicated than that," Burr countered. "It needs to be developed and protected to be worth anything. Property by itself is worthless. If you don't have a clear deed, and a good idea of what to do with it, you could never sell it at a decent price. How does it work for you? If you seize someone's property, is the property yours to sell? Where is your legal right to the property? Does the Transylvania Company allow you to keep whatever you want?"

"Well, I have a private arrangement with them, but yes, I am compensated based on what I turn over to them. I keep about a third of what I can get from people who are in debt to the Transylvania Company."

"How do you know you are getting a fair deal? Do you know what the property is worth to Transylvania? They may be giving you only a small amount of what it may be worth. If people are so easily willing to give up their property to settle debts, how do you know what you're getting, Jack?"

Jack took another beer and said, "Assemblyman Powell, a poor fellow like me is always a little in the dark about how the rich grab the wealth. I just want what's rightfully mine, based on the work I do. I know your brother has warrants and debts, and I'm supposed to collect one or the other for Transylvania. How that came about I'm not sure, but I heard a lot of talk at a card game in Alexandria."

"A card game? That could hardly transfer legal rights to property granted by the federal government. Did you see the warrants? Or a legal deed to the property? How do you plan to get them?"

"My methods are for me and my boys. Transylvania doesn't want to know or even care about how they get their property. We are small and insignificant to the grandees of the world, but we have to live too."

"Suppose I offered you an arrangement better than you would get from Transylvania? Could that change your methods? Would you be willing to talk about alternatives?"

Jack laughed out loud and said, "Sir, I'm always willing to talk."

Burr replied, "That's why we have politicians and general assemblies. We talk and talk and talk. We make our laws and we see that they are enforced. But most of what I do has to with protecting people from those who would prey on them in some way. You have an odd attitude toward landowning. Are you a landowner, Jack?"

Jack smiled and looked Burr straight in his face, saying, "By tomorrow I will be. Perhaps we should talk then."

Burr looked at Jack, who was well armed and physically fit. Burr was unarmed and overweight, but Burr knew the politics of the moment. "I hope you don't plan to do anything that's illegal. We have serious laws in Virginia governing land rights. We also support militias to enforce them."

"My land will be in Ohio."

"A friendly neighboring state. The Virginia General Assembly works well with the new state of Ohio. Washington did some surveying there. Washington was well known to my father, who served in the revolution. Washington saw to it that my father received the warrants he'd earned."

"Good for your father. Warrants aren't that special. They are like property deeds anywhere. If you want to keep them, you have to protect them and not gamble them away."

Burr looked at Jack, "Powell warrants belong to the Powells. Virginia will protect them."

Jack finished his beer and said to Burr, "Is this personal with you or a matter for the General Assembly?"

Burr finished his beer and replied, "There is no difference here. Virginia protects its own people against thugs and bandits. If you were one of us, we'd protect you."

"Not likely. The General Assembly protects its own and nobody else. Mr. Jefferson was the same. All that high-flying language about equality of the people, but he kept his slaves and had no use for ordinary working people either. When he had enemies, he hired the likes of me, but somehow couldn't find the cash to pay us when the deeds were done."

"Did you go after Mr. Burr? I suppose Jefferson would say you didn't do your job, since he's alive somewhere right now. Did Jefferson pay you for killing all those others, including the Indians?"

Walsh stood up and seemed angry, but it was unclear about what. "Are you accusing me of something, sir? I have committed no crime against anyone here, nor do I plan any such thing. My history of past work and payments has nothing to do with what I'm doing here. I have friends and relatives in Winchester who will support me. It's true I plan to collect a debt owed me, which I am sure is allowed in the great state of Virginia."

Burr replied, "These kinds or arguments should be settled in courts or in the legislature, not by armed gangs."

Jack smiled, "One man's gang is another's protection. Those who are not of the establishment can't expect fair treatment from courts and legislatures. If I was brought before a court, I'd be hung within a week and we both know it. There's no justice for ordinary men like me. We are here to try to equalize the situation. You know about equal rights for all the people, don't you?"

The timber of conversation seemed to be escalating, and just before Burr replied, Henry stepped behind the bar, furnished Jack with another beer and asked, "Will you and your friends be staying tonight? We'll have some beef stew ready in about an hour. My grandson will be taking over here shortly, and you are welcome to tell him of any of your needs."

Jack looked out at the late afternoon sun and said, "Yes, but we'll be leaving early for Winchester tomorrow, probably by daybreak. There are five of us."

Henry nodded, and pointed to the stair indicating that he had the space in the upstairs room. He then came out from behind the bar, put his arm on Burr's shoulder and pushed him out the back door.

Henry led Burr back to his house where Anna, the four teenagers and now Dave and John Powell were eating an afternoon dinner. Burr, very tired from the travel of the last days and now full of beer, greeted them all, sat down in a chair, and quickly fell asleep.

Henry spoke to the teenagers. "I have an idea where Billy is and there could be a fight. I think you all should go home early tomorrow and let the grandmothers know that Billy has many friends who will protect him. I'll be going out there with some of my neighbors. We are all militia."

Beth then spoke up. "But I want to talk to Billy and see him. I think we should go with you. I've been in the woods and can handle a pistol. I won't get in your way."

Burr slept and said nothing. Henry looked at him, replying, "Your father isn't cut out for a battle in the woods around Winchester. Would you and your brother go without him? I'm getting ready to leave in an hour or so to give Billy warning. We think we could be facing a large crowd, maybe a gang of fifteen or twenty. In the woods, that's a lot of people. Some could hide behind and up in trees, and they'll be well armed."

Beth asked, "How long will it take for you to get to Billy? And who are the people after him?"

Henry said, "It will take us two to three hours to get to where I imagine Billy's camped. We'll get there after nightfall and the woods are dark. Your father can explain this dispute better than I can. It's just that some people think they are entitled to own property, and they think nothing about taking it from people who they think are less worthy. That's partly what the revolution was about. We thought that we owned the land. We lived on it, built our farms and towns on it. The king and parliament thought they owned it and us besides. A lot of philosophical arguments were thrown about debating who the deserving ones are. We still have different sides to the argument."

John interrupted, asking, "You mean Jefferson and Burr? I guess the people out here will be for Burr. Maybe I would be too. In his own way, so is Father."

Beth thought a moment and then said, "I'm going with you, and I don't care what my father says. Billy is my uncle and I want to talk to him."

John looked at his father and said, "Billy's my uncle and I'll go. That's why Father insisted I come; he wouldn't be here except to talk to Billy about me for some reason. I think you are right about my father not being much use in the woods. I think he should be in a carriage all the way to Winchester and I should drive it. You'll have to tell me where in Winchester to go and how to get there."

Henry said, "There's a place on the main road called the Golden Sparrow. They'll have room and it isn't very far from where we'll be. Leave as early as you can if you want a chance to talk ahead of whatever this becomes."

"Could we go now? We could load Father in the back of the carriage with our bags. It might take three of us to do it, but he could sleep the whole way."

Bobby and John walked over to where Burr snored in the chair and then looked back at Henry, who laughed. "Wait a bit," Henry joked. "My neighbors will be here soon and they are better up to the task of moving a Virginia assemblyman."

Bobby said, "Henry, I should go with you to the campsite. My grandmother would be ashamed of me if I didn't go. Beth and I made it through the woods together, and I think I could be a help in the trees." He looked at Beth when he said this, and she became a little embarrassed.

"Well, get your things together and go out back and try out your pistols. When you see the neighbors, send them in here. Susan and Daniel can go back using the main road, and Dave will go with them and show them the way."

Anna said, "Yes, they'll take the cart and the mule. I have some knit hats and warm blankets for the grandmothers. Go straight to Mrs. Powell. Wait till the morning light before you go."

CHAPTER 27

MEETINGS IN WINCHESTER

WHEN JOHN AND Burr arrived at the Golden Sparrow that evening, they could see that the inn, much larger than the Black Eagle, entertained numerous guests. Large wagons, carriages, small carts, and horses were tied up at long railings surrounding the place.

Burr had slept most of the way and now felt rested. Before entering, he said to John, "Well, let's see if we can avoid a full-scale war. We didn't fight a revolution so that veterans could be cheated out of home and hearth."

John looked at his father. "Billy didn't fight in the revolution. Neither did Walsh. It's just a card game to them."

"Not so. Property outlives its owners. It has a provenance. The law respects deeds and honest claims that have evidence to support them. You don't get that in a card game."

"If you gamble and lose, you have to pay the price, even in Virginia."

"We don't know if Billy did any such thing. The claims here are muddy. Third parties, with nothing to do with Billy, are making the claims. They think they can strongarm their way to taking the property."

John looked at his father. "Not everyone wants to be a pioneer and settler. Many will give up their claims for the right price. Is Billy really a settler? He has no family or roots anywhere."

"He's a Powell and one of us. His property is Powell property. We're here to deal with Walsh. We have to figure out Walsh's price and offer it to him if he'll put down his guns."

John snorted but said nothing. They tied up their cart and entered the inn. Burr went directly to the bar while John found a small table in a dark corner and sat down.

Burr asked the bartender, "I'm looking for my brother, Billy Powell. Have you seen or heard from him?"

The dark-haired, heavy-set bartender had a small scar over one eye that made him look as if he were staring over the shoulder of the person to whom he was speaking. He had a deep gruff voice. "He was here two days ago with his friend George. They were expecting some friends to join them in the woods. Some men here from Alexandria are also looking for him. They are sitting out on the porch in the back. You might want to talk to them."

Burr motioned to John, who followed his father to the back porch. There they saw six tables, all but one occupied by four or more people. Two tall men in leather skins sat at the sixth. Burr recognized them as militia members from Alexandria.

Burr approached the two men. "How do you do, sirs? I'm Burr Powell, brother to Billy and Cuthbert Powell. I believe you are looking for my brother Billy."

The two men rose and shook hands with Burr and John, motioning them to sit. The taller of the two replied, "I'm Ed Hawkins of the Alexandria militia. This is Tom Perkins. We've been sent by Mr. Cuthbert Powell, our mayor, to bring back Jack Walsh for trial. There have been some complaints about him in Alexandria. We understand that Billy is in the woods waiting for trouble. We hope to head that off before anyone gets hurt."

John said, "Sir, I hope you can do that, but Walsh has a gang of fifteen or twenty. He should arrive here by tomorrow midday with five men and they plan to meet up with the others, possibly in the woods. It seems everyone knows where Billy is camped out."

Burr said, "Perhaps I can talk Walsh out of this confrontation. I'd also like a chance to talk to Billy before Walsh arrives. Could you take us out to Billy's campsite?"

"Well, we travel as a group. We are waiting for Walsh. I don't know how we can get you to the campsite. There are no roads and the woods are thick and dark. Paths are narrow and hard to see. Can you walk a mile, sir?"

"For my brother, I'll walk two miles. This is my son John. He'd like to speak with his uncle as well."

Ed looked at Burr. "Sir, I think you should rest a bit. Possibly your brother will be back here before evening and save you the trip. If Walsh will be here by tomorrow, we can't leave now."

Burr and John went inside and ordered two beers and the meal of the day. When they came back out to the porch, they could see that Ed and Tom had two additional militia men with them.

Burr approached Ed, who seemed to be the leader. "I'd really like a chance to talk to Walsh before things get out of hand. Wouldn't we all be better off if the gang gave up their guns?"

Ed shrugged. "I don't know if Walsh is a talker, but you have my blessing if that can be arranged."

While they spoke, they could see the wagon of Marcus the Magician approaching. They could also see two riders on horseback close behind him. The two riders seemed to hurry. As they came closer, John recognized his uncle as one of the riders. Shouting "Uncle Billy! Uncle Billy!" aloud, he jumped up and down on the porch.

Billy and George tied up their horses and climbed up onto the back porch where all the tavern patrons looked at them curiously. Billy shook hands with Burr and threw his arm around John, saying,

"What brings you two to these cold, dark woods? You don't look like fishermen to me."

George, standing right behind them, smiled and immediately turned to the militiamen. He and Ed became engrossed in conversation, with George explaining some locations, moving plates and cutlery around the small table to indicate something he'd been planning.

Marcus then climbed up on the porch; seeing John and Burr, he shouted, "How fine to see you here! Where are the young ladies? Louise enjoyed them very much."

Billy looked at Marcus and introduced himself. He said, "How do you do, sir? I'm Billy Powell, proud uncle to John here and his sister Beth, who is waiting back at our campsite. How did you come to know them?"

Marcus smiled, "Oh, that's a long story best told near a campfire. Miss Beth knows all and is highly favored by my bear Louise. John watched Louise just today. Wasn't she a marvel?! But wait, I need some refreshment."

With that, Marcus left the group and entered the tavern, where he ordered a beer and a bowl of fish chowder which he ate at the bar. He took a second tankard of beer back to the porch and there was approached by Burr.

"Sir, I saw your entertainment today and it was wonderful. My daughter is back at her uncle's campsite waiting for us. Would it be too much for you to take me to the campsite in your wagon? It's evidently not that far, but it's dark and I'm no rider on horseback. I'll be happy to give you twenty dollars for your trouble."

Marcus was astounded. "Twenty dollars? It would take me almost a year to make that much, but the woods are dangerous, are they not? And Louise will be difficult to control there. She loves the woods and will find joy with her baby playing about. I just got her back after a year of her roaming."

George heard this and came over to the group. "I would love to see your Louise and your entertainment and so would my men who are back at the campsite. People of my tribe almost worship bears and love them dearly. I promise you will not be in danger. I will post a sentry at your wagon and someone will watch Louise at all times. You won't have trouble finding the place as you can follow us."

George nodded to Billy and both motioned to John. They went back to their horses, while John threw a blanket over the back of the horse that had pulled Burr's carriage. He mounted the horse and came back to where Billy and George were waiting for him. Marcus went back to his wagon, a square, lumbering vehicle pulled by two mules. In a short while, the wagon was back at the tavern. Burr struggled to climb up to sit next to Marcus, but only an hour later the whole party disembarked at the campsite.

CHAPTER 28

CAMPSITE NEAR WINCHESTER

By THE TIME the party arrived, night had fallen. The woods, already very dark, seemed a mass of black with an occasional dark gray shadow. The sounds were of nocturnal animals, sorrowful, almost morose. A small fire lit up the cooking area and several men; Bobby and Beth sat around it huddled in blankets. Bobby wore the jacket Beth had given him earlier. The cold night air left Beth shivering despite the heavy blanket.

Marcus guided his wagon to the back of the clearing away from the fire. He jumped from the front of the rig to tie his two mules to small trees. By the time he'd secured the mules, he was surrounded by Beth, Bobby, Billy and George and about ten other men.

Beth saw Billy and immediately ran up to embrace him. He caught her and embraced her, saying "Well, another Powell family reunion. Your dad is in the wagon with your friend Louise the bear, I believe."

"Not so," said Burr, who'd managed to climb out of the wagon while Marcus was busy with the mules. "I've ridden with Marcus, who deserves our gratitude. The bear and her baby are asleep. I think the motion of the cart had something to do with that, and we are now on notice to keep her content and with us until Marcus can leave. We should take the time now to talk about what we expect will happen here."

Burr looked at George with a curious look on his face, which caused George to ceremoniously bow. George said, "Mr. Virginia assemblyman, you recognize me but can't quite place the face. I know I've changed, but not that much, I hope. My full name, to remind you, is George Morgan White Eyes. I am now chief of the Lenape tribe in Ohio and have been elected as a member of the Ohio legislative assembly. I am here to support my old friend Billy with my men and to escort him back to an Ohio courthouse where he can present his executed warrants and receive legal deeds to his property. We've been informed that the Transylvania Company seeks to seize the warrants, by force if necessary."

Burr laughed out loud and shook George's hand. He said, "Of course. I should have known immediately. We are all here for Billy as well. If the warrants are executed, does that mean they've been legally assigned to Billy?"

"Yes. They are legally his, and he's worked the land for these last five years. You are a member of the assembly. Isn't it true that no court in Virginia would grant his property rights to Transylvania now?"

"Transylvania is a large company with many friends in the Virginia courts and assembly. They are powerful and often get their way whatever the law. Are Walsh's interests the same as Transylvania's? Can he do something with warrants executed to someone else?"

George responded, "Transylvania employs a large legal staff and they've succeeded in transferring some warrants from other veterans' families by dealing with certain courts and judges in Virginia. Billy has to get out of here in one piece and back to Ohio to safeguard the property."

"I've spoken with Walsh once," Burr replied. "If I can offer him something, maybe we can settle this whole thing peaceably. You should also know that Cuthbert has sent out some militia to bring Walsh back to Alexandria on charges that have been brought against him there. There are at least four of them back at the Golden Sparrow and they are waiting for Walsh."

Billy, with one arm on John's shoulder and the other on Beth's, said, "Walsh won't be going to the Golden Sparrow. He has relatives in this region and will likely meet up with them before coming here. We estimate he'll have an army of over fifty by the time he adds all his cousins to the party he's brought with him."

George slapped Burr on the back. "How about you give a new assemblyman some advice while we let Uncle Billy speak with his niece and nephew and Bobby over there near the fire? Walsh isn't the only person with relatives, you know. We could have near a hundred, once we add up all the militia men from different locations, my men, and their relatives in these parts. Burr, we have to keep everyone talking so we can avoid people shooting at each other."

Billy, John and Beth moved over to the fire, which now was raging as new wood had been added. Billy said to John, "Beth tells me she loves the woods and would like to come back to Ohio with us. I don't think your mother would approve right now, but you're getting to an age where you can make some plans for the future. Have you thought about where you'd like to be and what you'd like to do?"

John crossed his legs as he sat down near the fire next to Bobby. Though only a year apart in age, they were physically quite different from one another. While sitting, they were not much different in height, but compared to John, Bobby was rugged. Bobby had powerful hands and arms from working on his parents' farm. John had darker hair, but his complexion paled compared to Bobby's. His shoulders were broader, but he'd clearly spent most of his young life indoors.

Beth asked John, "How did you manage with Father?"

"He slept the whole way in the back of the buggy with a heavy blanket thrown on him. When we got to the tavern, he was refreshed and in his element. He struck up a conversation with militiamen from Alexandria."

Billy heard the conversation. "Yes, your dad is a great talker, an orator even. I understand you'd like some words with me, and I know what your dad will want me to say. But I want to hear your side. What future do you think about, John?"

"Uncle Billy, I feel I'm being pushed into a decision before I'm ready. I'd like to study some and see more of the world than western Virginia before I make a major decision."

Bobby couldn't contain himself. "You are so fortunate to have this chance. Do you imagine what the future is like for someone like me? If I don't stay on my father's farm and learn his trade, I'll have nothing. Likely I'll just starve to death someday. I'll never get out of the woods of Virginia."

Beth looked at Bobby. "That's silly," she objected. "You are strong and resourceful. You could learn lots of trades, if you put your mind to it. My dad can help find you an apprenticeship somewhere."

"Not if my dad doesn't want that. He'll need a hand as he's getting older. My two brothers are little, and my sisters will marry and move away."

Billy looked at the three teenagers and remembered his own youth spent during the revolution. He sighed. "Yes, sometimes we can't really plan ahead, but we are who we are. I stayed back in Middleburg during the revolution and saw Washington in person a few times. He was for building a country and looked west. He was a great man in Virginia, but he saw a different and larger place as his country. He left a country for us to build."

John replied, "I'm not here for Washington, but my dad. You know that, Uncle Billy. He has something up his sleeve. He's ready to talk up a deal with Walsh and I don't want to know about it. Something in his head has me involved."

"Your dad is good at creating deals and so can George," Billy laughed. "What if such a deal eventually resulted in you coming out to Ohio? Would you object to that?"

John looked at Beth. "You would go, I know."

Billy said, "She's not going on her own at the age of fourteen without her parents' permission, and I know her mother. She'll have to wait."

Beth replied, "Can we talk to George? Maybe he has something to say about this."

Bobby looked into the fire and said, "Maybe I could go, if a chief and member of the legislature figures a place for me."

CHAPTER 29
PREPARATIONS AND DEALS

GEORGE AND BURR had moved to the back of the campsite where the pale light of the moon allowed them to see the ground and each other's faces. George spoke very quietly.

"We've looked over the place and have set up a route to bring in guns and ammunition that will be hard for them to stop. We will also position a few men in the trees; they'll be able to alert us as to when they are coming, and how many. We plan to surround them if we have a chance."

Burr replied, "You have the experience, but why should they cavalierly walk into the campsite, knowing how many men we have?"

George smiled and said, "Tomorrow at midday, Marcus and his bears will perform for us. We'll have a lot of joyous shouting and applause. The noise will carry through the woods, and they'll think we're here for a good time. They will march in carrying weapons when I'll take the stage and Marcus leads the bear away. I will invite Walsh to confer, while my men get the drop on his."

"Such a simple plan. So simple that lots of things can go wrong. What if they come in with guns blazing? Beth will be up on the stage and John not far away." Burr was worried.

George looked at Burr. "My men will surround the stage and will try to protect them. If you aim for John to come to Ohio, he needs to know what he's getting into. We are a rough new state."

Burr noticed that Beth, John and Bobby were approaching. He said, "Don't give them weapons. They'd only hurt themselves."

Beth spoke first. "George, what chance do we have to come into Ohio with you after this is over?"

George smiled and replied, "A very direct question. Do you speak for all three of you?'

Bobby replied, "I would very much appreciate knowing what opportunities would be available for me, though John here has some doubts about going."

They were now standing in a circle, and Burr moved back so the teenagers could have a better look at George. George was dressed in leather-skins and looked tall, thin and powerful. He carried himself like a chief, though he wore no feathers. He had painted two red stripes on each of his cheeks in preparation for the battle and looked fierce. His speech was educated and articulate.

"My dear young men and young lady, I have discussed the matter with your uncle and plan to continue the conversation with Burr here. I plan to travel to Middleburg when we are finished here, while Billy moves on to Ohio. We can't be certain how everything will play out yet, but I will have your interests in my mind and we can talk later. For you, Beth, think about what your mother will say and how she would feel if you left home at your age. John and Bobby, the same goes for you. Are you ready to be settlers, or should you first be apprenticed and learn some skills, or attend a college and study science or the law? Just think about all this. For now, pay attention to how we set the stage for tomorrow. We play a dangerous game and don't want anyone to be hurt."

Three of George's Lenape men approached and George excused himself. The three men were taller and larger than George and each had three yellow stripes painted on each cheek. They wore leather-skins and carried rifles. Burr said, "Let's go to the fire and keep out of the way of the militia. It's late. Time to pitch tents for sleeping."

Burr and the boys went toward the fire while Beth walked quickly to Marcus' wagon where the bears slept. She spoke with Marcus and understood what he planned to do for his show the next day. She then came back to the campfire and crawled into her small tent, but was too excited to sleep. She was up at daybreak, anxious to help set up the stage and feed the bears.

CHAPTER 30

CONFRONTATION IN THE WOODS

THROUGHOUT THE NIGHT, Billy, George and four of the men from Ohio took turns keeping watch. Ten men, mostly George's relatives living near Winchester, positioned themselves in the woods under high trees which they planned to climb early the next morning. They'd agreed on whistle signals to indicate the approach of Walsh and his men.

Billy and George wanted no surprises. Burr and the three teenagers were to stay with Marcus near the stage. The stage, though on a small platform, abutted a pebbled path leading to Marcus' wagon in the rear. Armed Lenape fighters would be positioned near the stage at every corner and along the path to the wagon. Beth would be helping Marcus with the bears and George asked the young people to leave their weapons with Billy.

John and Burr were happy to give their guns away. Beth insisted on keeping a pistol, and Bobby refused to hand over his rifle which had been given to him by one of the Logan boys back at the Logan farm. Beth was determined to defend herself if necessary this time. Bobby felt confident and was certain he could shoot straight with the rifle, at least at close range. Burr and Billy decided not to argue, but insisted that the teenagers stay behind the line of fighters, along with Burr, Marcus and the bears.

At daybreak, the party lined up for a breakfast of cooked oats, bacon and coffee, prepared by five women and two men from the local area. The women, armed with pistols and rifles, were included in the military planning. Some were to surround the stage, others to find places in the nearby woods. Fighters came to breakfast in groups of six and eight, with Billy, George, Marcus and the teenagers eating last. George counted his fighting force at over one hundred and twenty, about ninety men and thirty women.

Marcus wore bright silks in spectacular red, blue and yellow colors. He wore a red satin turban and an embroidered robe with deep pockets on both sides. He spoke to George: "Your people will enjoy the show. Louise will be delighted to perform now that Beth is here. I've given them both matching gold and blue sashes to wear; both have them tied around their necks and make quite a pair. Beth also has a belt tied around her waist with bags of treats for the bears."

Burr asked, "Did she keep her pistol too? Has she loaded it? I worry if she's jumping around wearing a loaded pistol."

"She's anxious to be able to defend herself if anything should happen," George assured Burr. "She had a bad experience in the woods and there's not much use for a pistol that isn't loaded. She'll have to be careful moving around. She's old enough and understands this. My cousin Red Feather instructed her how best to pull it out of her belt and aim it."

Burr shook his head in worry and Billy slapped him on the back. Billy said, "Worry doesn't help. This is what they came for. This confrontation will be something to remember, like we remember Valley Forge and Washington. Though it was harsh and no battle, we came out of it with a clearer view of who we were and what we wanted. We had a leader and we knew where we wanted to go. This time we go to Ohio. Washington would be proud of these young people."

Burr said nothing, but stood up and walked slowly back to the stage where Beth, Bobby and John were watching Marcus perform a few card tricks. Some of the Lenape had taken their positions, and soon a crowd of nearly two hundred came shuffling around the stage. Onlookers included men, women and children mostly from nearby areas and included George's fighting force who blended in without easily being identified.

The show began with Beth beating a drum. Marcus followed with a blast on his trumpet, followed by songs accompanied by him on guitar. He then followed with a few card tricks, and soon there were shouts of "Where's the bear?"

Beth turned around and walked quickly to get Louise and Blackbeard from the wagon. She unshackled the small cage, but soon heard the sounds of footfalls behind her. She turned and saw Bobby and George's cousin Red Feather. In the trees above, she knew at least three Lenape fighters were hidden. She managed to get Louise and Blackbeard out of the cage when she heard a whistling sound from above.

The Lenape had spotted a party of Walsh's followers making their way through the woods. Beth wasted no time in pushing Louise and Blackbeard forward to where Marcus waited for them. The great mother bear, wearing her bright silk sash, took the stage, but instead of climbing the ladder, she immediately turned right, jumped into the crowd, and raced toward a man standing at the edge of the wood. He had a visible bandage on his head. When he saw the bear, he turned and ran. Before she could disappear into the woods, two Lenape fighters moved in front of Louise and shook rattles that stopped her. They shouted to Beth, "Start with the baby bear. His mother will come to you."

Beth took Blackbeard by the paw and led him to Marcus, who

helped him up one of the small ladders. Beth fed the cub sweets throughout the process. Within five minutes, Louise was back on the stage and Beth moved behind the ladder that held Blackbeard.

The loud popping sound of nearby gunfire could be heard and the crowd divided in two. Unarmed onlookers moved toward the stage, instructed to do so by armed fighters. The fighters quickly formed a line to protect the perimeter. The fighting line around the stage numbered more than forty carrying loaded rifles.

As the crowd shuffled their positions, Beth left the stage, followed closely by Blackbeard. She took a sweet for the cub out of a bag hanging from her belt, but felt an arm on her shoulder pulling at the sash that had been tied around her neck. She let out a short cry and groped for her pistol. She didn't see who was pulling her and she determinedly tried to hold Blackbeard's paw. The little bear, who weighed more than she did, pulled away and ran to his mother, who was being shepherded by Marcus toward the wagon.

Beth managed to turn to see a red-haired man waving a long knife in the air. She pulled out her pistol, forgot to aim and pulled the trigger. The blast from the pistol was loud and caused her to fall back with her shot going somewhere into the air.

She was surprised to see the red-haired man fall to the ground screaming. She knew she hadn't shot the man. He'd been shot in the lower thigh from the rear by Bobby, who'd been waiting at the edge of the wood with his rifle.

Red Feather came over to Bobby and smiled, saying, "Good shot. He'll need some help, but can still talk." Red Feather motioned to two Lenape fighters, who lifted the wounded man and brought him up on the stage where two women looked at the red-haired man's wound. They tended to him quickly and he lost little blood as they extracted the round bullet that wasn't deeply embedded in his flesh. He had no broken bones.

The people who remained near the stage could hear loud

shuffling noises, some screams, and a few gunshots from the nearby woods, but gradually the noises diminished. In less than an hour, George and Billy led most of the Walsh Winchester force in a group out of the woods to a clearing facing the front of the stage. Walsh's supporters had given up their weapons and stood in a crowd guarded by George's men and the militias of three counties.

Red Feather spoke from the stage. "I believe we have Mr. Walsh here. I understand that we've had no thefts and no killings, so there is no need for the militias to get into action. No laws have been broken in this county. Mr. Billy Powell, Assemblyman Burr Powell, George Morgan White Eyes, myself and Mr. Walsh, with people of Mr. Walsh's choice, will confer quietly for a while. We will then join members of the militias in the large tent near the cooking area. My Winchester cousins are tending to Mr. Walsh's wounds. Marcus has agreed to continue with the show for our guests while we move to the rear of this clearing to wait for Mr. Walsh to confer."

Beth, fighting tears, moved toward the stage where she found her father. Burr immediately embraced her and patted her back. He held her while she gulped deep breaths. He said, "Two close calls in just two days. Are you sure you want to go to Ohio?"

Beth could barely speak, but when she heard Red Feather, she straightened up and said, "Father, I can go west as well as anyone. I'm not afraid and I can defend myself. They need me on the stage now." She turned and ran to the stage where she stood next to Louise, both their bright silk sashes blowing in the breeze.

CHAPTER 31

CONFERENCES IN THE WOODS

B Y THE TIME the group of leaders convened in a small clearing behind the stage near Marcus' wagon, they numbered twelve. Walsh insisted that his wife, two cousins and his uncle accompany him. He expected his wife and uncle to do most of the talking.

Jack's uncle, Bill Walsh, a short stubby man, had lost his hair, limped along with a cane, and spoke in a deep, gruff voice. Jack's wife Amy stood as tall as Jack; if she weren't dressed in leathers and ready for war, she would have been considered pretty. Limber and graceful, with dark hair and dark eyes, she was about thirty years of age. She'd been part of other confrontations and acted as spokesperson in group meetings many times.

Billy sat down on the bare ground. To his right sat George and to his left, Burr. Red Feather sat next to Burr. Two men from Ohio stood behind them. None of them were armed.

Jack, with the help of Amy, sat down. Amy sat to his right, his Uncle Bill on his left, and three cousins stood behind them. Seven people formed a circle and looked at each other. Five others were onlookers.

Jack was pleased to be sitting as his bandaged leg still hurt. Looking at Billy, he began. "Well, you have me hurting, but I think I have many more relatives in the Winchester region than you and your friends here."

Red Feather stood and walked over to Amy. He had a broad smile on his face and said, "Mrs. Walsh, you may not remember me but I attended your wedding here in Winchester. I didn't wear my war stripes and you were dressed differently too. Your mother and my sister are in-laws, married to Lenape brothers. We were a party of twenty or so at your wedding."

Amy looked at Red Feather, but could not recognize him. "Sir, I'm sure you are speaking the truth, but I can't be certain about anyone who came to my wedding celebration. We had almost the whole county at one time or another. If you say we've met before and are related, I'm happy to know that, as will my mother. Jack should certainly be happy to know this. I hope we can reach a peaceable settlement here."

Jack groaned as he heard the conversation and starting rubbing his injured leg. Amy slapped his hand, pushing it off his leg and said for all to hear, "We could also have another fight so my Jack here would end up without any leg to stand on."

George motioned to Red Feather and stood up to whisper to him. Red Feather was older than George, probably near fifty, but he was also taller and very fit. The two shared a facial resemblance with relatively dark skin and eyes and somewhat prominent cheekbones, though Red Feather's hair, tied behind his neck, was gray. George still looked youthful with very black hair. After a short conversation, they sat down again. George spoke, mainly addressing Jack. "I do not know details about this dispute, but I do know that my friend here, Billy Powell, has been working his land in Ohio these past five years. I don't understand how you can feel entitled to his property."

Jack responded, "I represent the Transylvania Company and they have instructed me to collect the Powell warrants, based on debts owed to them by third parties well known to Mr. Billy Powell."

Burr smiled at Jack. "Tell us, Jack, why you think Transylvania feels they should have the Powell warrants."

"That's not for me to say. They have lawyers and politicians sending out instructions."

Billy retorted, "Are your relatives from Winchester here for Transylvania?"

Amy looked at Jack and advised, "Well, time to start talking."

Jack just sat quietly.

Burr continued, "Our brother Cuthbert, mayor of Alexandria, has sent militia to bring Jack back on charges of defrauding people in Alexandria City. These militia men know nothing of Transylvania. Besides, Cuthbert knows the president of Transylvania well. They are neighbors in Alexandria."

Jack grew red in the face and spurted, "These are false charges. I've never defrauded anyone. If Transylvania made a deal, they have turned me out to the wolves and they know they're doing it."

Amy put her arm on Jack's shoulder as Burr continued speaking. "You know that Transylvania cares nothing about the people working for them. They come and go at will. But you thought this was a personal debt to you, didn't you?"

"Yes. Mr. Simpson, well known to Mr. Billy Powell, owes me five hundred dollars, lost fairly in a card game well witnessed in Alexandria. Mr. Billy Powell, present at the game, is Mr. Simpson's partner; isn't that so?"

Billy looked at Walsh, "Have we ever had anything to do with one another? How do I come to owe you anything?"

George interrupted. "Sir, we are meeting to see if we can tell the militias to disband. I am George Morgan White Eyes. Some of you may have heard of my father, a great friend and supporter of George Washington and the founding of this country. I believe he was well known here in the Winchester region. I officially have taken the name of George Morgan White in the Ohio Congress, but I remain chief of the Lenape tribe in Ohio. I also have been elected to represent my county, Adams County, in the Ohio House of Representatives. I can assure you that the warrants for Powell land were legally assigned to Billy Powell and have been recognized in a federal court in Virginia. You and Transylvania have no legal right to Billy Powell's land."

Bill Walsh responded, "Isn't that for a court to decide? Isn't it true that Jack would have no chance at a fair hearing in Alexandria with all the powers there aligned with Billy's brothers, Burr and Cuthbert?"

Billy looked at Jack and quietly said, "How can we reach an agreement without arms? What do you want, Jack? Is there a way we can arrive at a compromise we can all live with?"

Jack looked at Amy and Uncle Bill. They began to speak quietly and sometimes raised their voices to unintelligible shouts. Several times, Uncle Bill angrily stood up and walked around the circle. When he sat down, Amy did most of the talking, with Jack shaking his head yes and no alternately throughout the conversation. Finally, Uncle Bill stayed down and Amy spoke to the group.

"We are not in the business of defrauding and strong-arming people out of their property, though Jack has gone to great lengths to create a reputation for that. This reputation got Transylvania interested in him. On the other hand, we are owed a sizeable debt from a person with close connections to Billy Powell. Billy, do you question that?"

Burr tried to stop Billy from speaking, but Billy quickly responded. "Mrs. Walsh, I saw that card game, but was not part of it. There was discussion of investment in some building in Alexandria or Leesburg with which I have no connection. My arrangement with Simpson was to get him to come out to Ohio and help settle my land. He was ready to purchase some farming acres near the town of Cincinnati. I never agreed to accept his debts as mine."

Jack asked, "Has Simpson put up his investment for your acreage?"

Billy spoke, "No, but we expect he will bring the cash with him when he comes out to Ohio, probably before the planting season. I expect him and his family in six or eight weeks or so."

"So, you aren't certain you'll be paid by him, are you?"

"My family has known his family all my life. My father and his father were early supporters of Washington and had a long and happy friendship. I trust John Simpson."

"Well, if you trust him that much, pay me the equivalent of five hundred dollars, and get the money back from him when you see him."

Billy looked at George who then looked at Red Feather. Burr simply shook his head and whispered to Billy.

After a few minutes, George spoke, "That may settle a debt, but it won't satisfy Transylvania or the Alexandria militia. Perhaps we can reach an agreement that will satisfy everyone. I am prepared to offer you and your wife a home along the Ohio, in exchange for an agreement from you to be my protection for times I have to visit the capital. Ohio today is not a pleasant and peaceful place. You and your family may want to discuss this. The state is now trying to determine where the capital city should be located. It's been in Chillicothe, but now has moved to Zanesville. The roads are rough and the tribes up north are planning a confederation to push new settlers out. The roads are dangerous. We have a small armory in Adams County, but we need experienced fighting men to organize our defense. You are experienced with weapons and gunfights. If you agree to come back to Ohio with Billy and my men, I'm sure we can find you a business partner in the town. Numerous new businesses are opening now. You would start out by working for me for a salary, and I'll advance you the money for investment in whatever new business you choose. That should be at least five hundred dollars."

Jack, surprised to hear the offer, looked at Amy, who had a smile on her face. She said, "Who will tell the Alexandria militia that they needn't bother us?"

Burr responded, "I will take that responsibility. I'd hoped that my son John would go to Ohio with Billy as well, but George has convinced us to wait a bit. George will be returning to Middleburg with me and we will see Cuthbert and the Simpsons about the arrangement together. Everything will be cleanly arranged. Jack won't be a wanted man in Virginia. I believe we have ways of dealing directly with Transylvania."

Amy, Jack and Uncle Bill conferred for a bit and ended with Uncle Bill saying, "We think this is a reasonable offer, but probably Jack and Amy should go to Ohio as soon as possible. What if the militia changes its mind, or doesn't accept? Tell them Jack was taken into town to be bandaged up properly, but he and Amy should just get away."

Red Feather stood up and said, "I and five of my men can leave right now. With all these people still here watching Marcus and the bear, the militia will never know that we've gone. Do you have things you want to take with you? "

Amy responded, "No, I have our savings with me on my belt, and we have very little property of our own. We've been living with my mother. I can get our guns, if it's all right with you."

Red Feather replied, "We'll give you rifles and pistols for the journey. We'll make a crutch for Jack and carry some clean bandages for his leg. Once we clear the woods, some of the journey will be by raft and ferry where he'll be able to sit or lie down." Red Feather motioned to Amy to come to the edge of the wood; in a few minutes, five Ohio men had assembled along with eight horses and a mule tied to a wagon. Twenty minutes later, Jack, Amy, Red Feather and the men had disappeared into the woods.

CHAPTER 32

BARGAINING
WITH MILITIAS

URR STRUCK UP a conversation with Bill Walsh and together they walked to the tent occupied by leaders of the three militias—from Alexandria, Winchester and Henry Silver and his neighbors from the nearby counties. They were followed closely by Burr, Billy and George.

When they got to the tent, Burr recognized Henry Silver and Ed Hawkins of the Alexandria militia; Bill recognized several men from Winchester. The militia men were deeply engrossed in a game involving the tossing of small flat stones in various arranged piles. The game had a complex scoring system and Henry Silver acted as scorekeeper. With every toss, there were shouts and groans.

Burr and Billy waited near the players till the game seemed to be completed, while George stayed back near the entrance to the tent. The tossing stopped and one of the players from Winchester received congratulations and small payments from all onlookers. The friendly atmosphere seemed to contradict the reasons they all had come. An hour earlier, they had been armed and ready to shoot at one another.

Burr introduced himself and Billy, saying, "Thank you all for coming. My brother Billy and I are grateful to all for your concern and support in this difficult time. As you know, Ohio faces warfare from the northern Indian tribes that do not recognize our new country. Our President Madison in Washington still faces threats from the British, who believe the revolution never happened while they kidnap and impress our seamen. My own son has spoken of joining the navy, but he's young and for now he's still here. I can tell you I advised against it, but I'm afraid he'll see war again one way or another. Whichever way we look, by land or sea, there is war and violence. Now is a time for all of us to remember we are Americans and have to work together."

Burr had an audience now. His warm tenor voice rang out and he spoke clearly and with emotion. He'd had much success convincing legislators in the Virginia General Assembly to his point of view on matters of policy, and he used his speaking skills in full force for this group of thirty men.

Burr continued his speech, referring to Washington and the need to grow the country peaceably, and concluded by saying, "We have just spoken with Jack and Amy Walsh and they have reached an understanding with Billy. I am certain that our brother Cuthbert and the Alexandria authorities will agree with the arrangement. Billy has no dispute with anyone here or in Winchester."

Ed asked, "We have a warrant for the arrest of Jack Walsh and are instructed to bring him back to Alexandria with us. We left him in your custody because of his wound. What shall we do about the warrant?"

Billy responded, "Jack and I no longer have a dispute, and if you are here on my account, you can tell the Alexandria authorities that the warrant is based on false information. I will be happy to accompany you to make this report to Cuthbert and the Alexandria City Council."

"But shouldn't Jack also come?"

Bill Walsh responded, "We've taken Jack into town to better dress his leg. He likely won't be able to travel for a while, and if Alexandria doesn't need him that will save him the journey."

Ed looked at his new friends from the Winchester militia and Henry Silver. Henry, though sleepy looking, was alert and spoke up. "We are here as militia and all of us have farms and businesses that need our attention. If it's a piece of paper that worries you, surely Burr of the Virginia General Assembly and Cuthbert of the Alexandria City Council can take care of that. You'll have Billy Powell to confirm the truth. What more do you need? Let me add that I know it's a long way to Alexandria. Please come back with me to the Black Eagle and spend a day of rest. We have good fishing nearby and it will make your journey home more pleasant."

Burr added, "And please ask Cuthbert to provide compensation for your day's work and tavern fees. This visit to the Winchester woods shouldn't cost you anything. I'll be happy to send an official request from the General Assembly to that effect."

Ed walked around the tent and motioned to the men who'd come with him from Alexandria. They left the tent where they could speak privately. When they emerged, they could see that Louise the bear was performing before a large crowd and her brightly colored sash was waving in the wind.

The men walked back to a large tree where they could confer privately. Ed asked the others, "What do you all think? We are four and they are over a hundred. We'll get no help from Henry Silver or the Winchester crowd. Jack is safely away someplace."

Two of the men responded immediately. "Let's go home. The deal is clear. If they don't have an argument, why are we here anyway?" The other militiaman nodded his head in agreement.

After less than ten minutes, the Alexandria militia reentered the tent and signaled to Henry that they accepted the deal and his invitation to stay a day at the Black Eagle. Coming back with them would also be Billy, George, Burr, Beth, John and Bobby. Henry laughed, saying, "My house hasn't been so full since my seven children had birthday parties there. We managed then and will manage now. Anna will be very happy. We should get going."

George, pleased with the outcome, said "We'll have to wait till Marcus is finished. Beth, John and Bobby have been enlisted into the entertainment."

The militia men left the tent and wished each other well. After retrieving their guns and other equipment, Billy, Burr and George waited for Marcus to finish. At the end of the show and after long howls and cheers and applause, George approached Marcus. He said, "A wonderful show. Have you ever thought to come to Ohio? We are growing quickly and need shows and entertainment. We might be able to build you a more permanent showplace than your wagon. I'm sure you'll have enough customers to keep a permanent show going. We could put up a tent so you can perform in the winter, and you could have a house to live in."

Marcus looked at George. "That sounds wonderful, but how could I cross the great river? Louise can swim, but alas, I cannot do it that way."

"If you go with my men now, they know of a place with a ferry that will take you and your wagon across. When you get to Cincinnati or Adams, you must ask for Red Feather. He and I have discussed the need for a theater or circus. He'll know where to direct you."

Marcus smiled, "I've avoided war and violence, but it has always found me. I can't tell you how many times I've been attacked and robbed while working for myself. Louise has saved my life more than once. I thank you for the offer. Will you be coming?"

George responded, "No, I have business in Middleburg just now, but I'm pleased that you will go to Ohio. I'll look for you on my return."

PART THREE
MIDDLEBURG AND ALEXANDRIA

CHAPTER 33
WAITING FOR NEWS

A FTER BURR LEFT, Sally took to her bed saying she was too tired to do anything. The old woman ran a fever, looked very pale, and Jane worried about her. Nancy stayed at the Middleburg house, prepared cold compresses for Sally, and did some cooking and mending. Dorothy went home, anxious to hear news of the grandchildren.

The first day Sally stayed in bed, Jane prepared some chicken broth and spoon-fed her mother several times. For most of the day the old woman slept. Jane tried to put damp cloths on Sally's head, but Sally refused them while accepting cold compresses from Nancy.

After two days of illness, Sally seemed to recover and got out of bed. She ate a light breakfast of cooked oats and some berries and asked Jane, "How are you doing with the essay about Leven? Did Cuthbert or Burr say anything about it?"

Jane felt great relief at seeing her mother returning to her normal self. She smiled and went back to the darkest corner of the kitchen where she found the great box holding Leven's papers. She took out the essay and several letters she'd been reading.

She said to her mother, "Cuthbert read it carefully, as did Burr when he was here. They said little, as it's not finished. You remember we got as far as Valley Forge? Where do you think we should go next?"

Sally replied, "If this is really about Leven, you need to tell how he was when times were good as well as when he faced troubles. You have to capture who he was and why he felt the way he did. He talked to me and you children. You know what he used to say, whether it's written in those letters or not."

"Yes, not just how he reacted to things, but what he believed," Jane added. "What he wanted us to learn from him and his life experiences. We can never know what our young people think and believe. It probably would be instructive for them to understand their grandfather."

Sally thought for a few minutes and then said, "Tell where he came from and his morality. He had the philosophy of the revolution, but also religion. He really believed that language saying all men are created equal. Though he worshipped in many churches, he remained a Quaker in his heart and always inquired as to how the Quakers were being treated."

"He never admitted being Quaker; always said he was Episcopal."

"He had to if he wanted to marry me and get his hands on my dowry. My family, the Harrisons, were important in the eastern part of the state and strict supporters of the established religion. Leven needed their approval and a wedding before an Episcopal minister to marry me."

"Did you care about the religion? Did you make demands on Father?"

"No, I didn't and he knew it. We satisfied my parents and he became an Episcopal for them. We never attended a Quaker service together. You and the rest were baptized in Episcopal churches by Episcopal ministers. All our weddings were Episcopal, except for Cuthbert, who married a Baptist. In later years, I know Leven attended Quaker meetings from time to time, and I think his ideas of equality of all people came more from Quaker teachings than anything Jefferson ever wrote. He never agreed to keep slaves, though many landowners around us had slaves either in the house or the field. You know, Quakers were persecuted in many places, especially in the north. Leven always took an interest in the welfare of Quakers."

Jane continued to leaf through the documents as she said, "He wrote many letters but he never put his philosophy in writing for other people to know where he stood on things. You can see what he stood for through bits and pieces. Most of his letters and those he received are about illnesses, deaths, attacks by Indians, and payments for this and that. He was meticulous about paying what he owed and receiving what was owed him."

Sally sat back and Nancy brought her a cup of tea. Nancy inquired, "No word yet from the west? Dorothy should be back now any time. Are we speaking of Indian attacks and Leven?"

"We were thinking about where to go next, to give the reader a sense of who Leven really was and what sorts of letters would show that," Jane answered. "Mother mentioned religion as part of it."

Nancy weighed in, adding, "Well, that's a part of all of us, isn't it? Even Washington accepted the idea of a Creator, but to him all religions were equal. He meant it when he said we were all the same, and he freed his slaves in his will. Mr. Leven thought actions showed your beliefs and he acted when he had to. He believed in order, in a strong government to keep the country safe, and a court system to protect people and property."

At that moment, Dorothy entered the kitchen, a little out of breath. "Have I missed something? You'll be happy to know, Nancy, that Daniel and Susan will be arriving here by tomorrow or the next day along with Dave, Henry Silver's grandson. I received this news from my son-in-law who came back from the Black Eagle the short way, through Logan's farm. They are taking the main road and may stop to fish or something, but they are apparently fit and healthy and full of stories to tell. Mr. Burr Powell, his children, Billy Powell, and a load of armed men are on their way to the Winchester woods. I doubt we'll know more about what's happened for a few more days, maybe a week."

Nancy looked at Dorothy and said, "I guess Bobby stayed with the Powells too. He's a brave boy. We should say a prayer for all of them."

Dorothy whispered a few words to herself and then looked up, saying, "Let's not think about all of this. I didn't want to interrupt you. Have you more about Leven?"

Jane didn't want to raise the issue of Indian attacks as she thought it would add to everyone's anxiety. She'd found a letter she thought made her point about Leven. "Remember Father's laments about the hatter? Here is a piece of a letter he wrote to Burr in 1776:

"My brother writes me that the Hatter has run away, and desires to know whether he is to give up the Hatts which were left in the shop. I would by no means keep from a man what was his own. It will be difficult, however, to know who these Hatts were made for. The Hatter had wool from me to make 8 or 9 Hatts; if they have not been received, the probability is that many of them were made out of my wool; at any rate, I ought not to be the only loser."

"Yes, I remember it well," Dorothy laughed, "and that was Mr. Leven, very particular about accounts and not wanting to be cheated. Did he say something about justice there?

Jane laughed. "Yes, he finishes by announcing that when he returns, 'I will do equal justice.'"

"Oh, those were fighting words with him," Sally smiled. "He said that many times."

Jane continued, "Here's another long letter to Burr from 1791. Burr lived in Kentucky then and wasn't yet elected to the General Assembly. Leven issues long instructions to Burr as to how to negotiate with Mr. Hite over the disposition of some land, evidently in Kentucky near where Burr lived. He tells Burr, '... where you are at a loss, take advice and observe that, in all kinds of business ... coolness and caution is indispensably Necessary. I will give you another adage, more flies are caught with a Spoonful of Honey than a Gallon of Vinigar.'"

"Oh, yes. I remember that one," laughed Dorothy. "He especially held that back for Billy. Do you think it affected Billy in any way? Burr and Cuthbert really never needed to hear that. They were always diplomatic."

Jane said, "But there was more to Father than that. Here's another long letter to Burr written in 1799 when Father served in the U. S. Congress. Father was a loyal Federalist and supported the Constitution and the idea of strong central government. A Mr. John Taylor of Caroline evidently gave a flamboyant speech advocating states' and individual rights and a decentralized Federal government. Father describes him in this letter as 'a mad dog foaming at the mouth.'"

"Well, think of what we'd been through with the Articles of Confederation," noted Sally. "There was no money anywhere and Leven described the printing of paper money as laughable. Everyone distrusted everyone. Some of the states stopped trading with each other. We'd won a war, but didn't have a country when we remained decentralized. It was Washington and the Constitution that brought us together."

Nancy said, "That stayed with Mr. Leven all his life. The need for a strong government that would give us order and equal justice."

Jane said, "Yes, equality and justice were Father's principles. In this long 1791 letter, Father wrote about the new Kentucky government's power to tax land and is very detailed about how payments should be made. He also insists that Burr understand that 'after the Separation is complete and the New government takes place . . . You cannot bring slaves . . . to this State, they would by our laws be intitled to Freedom.'"

"Leven in this letter showed concern that Burr or someone he knew might bring slaves into Virginia, which had banned the importation of slaves. Leven strongly supported the new law and new government of Virginia," Sally shared.

Jane noted that Leven specifically pointed out in this letter that Thomas Jefferson was no longer Governor of Virginia.

CHAPTER 34

MORE ABOUT INDIANS

THE NEXT DAY, Sally felt much better and decided to clean up the vegetable garden. She pulled some weeds, watered the new plantings, and replanted some corn and green beans. After a few hours, she went back to the porch where she found Jane.

Jane had spent the morning milking their three cows and feeding the chickens and was pleased to be sitting down again. Next to Jane's chair, Hamilton, her pet beagle, sat lapping water from a bowl. He was eying the two yellow house cats, Nip and Tuck, who'd also come out to sit on the porch under a small, round, wooden table. The front door to the house was left open for easy access by people and pets.

Sally sat down on a rocking chair and said, "Should we go further with the essay? I'm too tired to do anything else."

"I suppose so. We all have our thoughts on Burr, Billy and the children. I'd forgotten till yesterday that Burr had actually lived in Kentucky and traveled to the edge of some great rivers."

"Yes, he wasn't married and not so fat and slow on his feet. I think he loved it in a way, but overall it was a frightening experience for him. He lived very close to where the Indians roamed, and he wrote

Leven about it. He's always hated physical violence. In Kentucky, he saw the results up close."

"Let's have some refreshments. I'll look out what we have about the Indians, but remember this essay is about Leven, not Burr. Also, remember White Eyes was an Indian too, and we all respected him, as did Washington."

"I think we'll all feel better when we grow some confidence that Burr is in a place where he knows what he's doing. He's Leven's son, after all. So is Billy. What a difference between two boys. What do you make of that?"

Jane thought a bit and said, "Honestly, I think Billy was first and always treated as special. He never needed to be political about anything. He just went out and did what he pleased. At the same time, he shared Father's principles. He was all for Washington, the Constitution and equality, but for him it was a sort of game, something to cheer for. Burr understood it differently. He's always been about making the deal by finding the spoonful of honey for everyone. Billy is all vinegar when he has a dispute over something. I'm glad Burr's gone into the woods for Billy, though I don't know why he took John and Beth."

Jane went inside the house and found Nancy and Dorothy in the kitchen busy with baking. Dorothy said, "We'll be feeding a few youngsters pretty soon. We thought a few meat and chicken pies and some sweet things would be appreciated. We could try some ourselves for our supper."

Jane replied, "What a good idea. You might also want to put the visitors to work at things. We won't have two young men around here for long. When you have a chance, come out to the porch. Mother and I will have something to drink now and we'll go back to Leven's essay." Jane took a pitcher of apple cider and two mugs and went back to the porch.

An hour later, the four women sat in large wooden chairs that circled the small round table on the wide porch which was shaded by two large elm trees. The dog still sat next to Jane and the two cats remained under the table. The weather had turned sunny and warm and the women looked forward to an afternoon of rest.

Nancy began, saying, "Daniel, Susan and Dave won't know much about what's happening in Winchester. I think we should keep them here until the rest of the group arrives, which can't be more than a few days longer. Besides, we thought of repairing the fence near the horse barn now that the summer is coming. With the three of them here, they might want to go for a ride now and then, and it will be nice to have a decent place to keep the horses outside of the barn."

Sally and Dorothy nodded their heads in agreement, but Jane said, "Let them relax first and tell us their stories. They might not be up to work right away, and I'm sure they'll be happy to be fed and have a place indoors to sleep. Likely they'll like the idea of fixing the fence and getting some riding in. Maybe also a little fishing in the creek?"

Jane shuffled some papers and then said, "Mother and I remembered that Burr lived in Kentucky for a while and I have a few letters he and some of his neighbors in Kentucky wrote to Father from that time. These are from the 1780s, before the Constitution and before Kentucky became a state:

"August 1783, from Christopher Greenup to Leven, 'More Indian tribes have arrived in peace but three murders have occurred by the Indians. The Cohee Indians are trying to drive settlers away.'

"September 1784, from Christopher Greenup to Leven, 'Savages have murdered dozens, including Walker Daniel, an Attorney General and the only other attorney in the county besides myself.'

"June 1785, from Cuthbert Harrison to Leven, 'Travels along the Monongahela River to Fort Pitt. The Indians were unfavorable, but the wives proved the greatest of heroines.'

"July 1786, from J. Hite to Leven, 'We have been much distressed by the Indians, and as usual your unfortunate friend shares a great Burthen of it. My brother Abraham Wounded abt the 1ˢᵗ of March with 2 balls in his thigh and lies very poorly yet with his wounds.'"

Jane looked up to see the impact of the latest reading on the older women. They didn't respond immediately, but looked at each other and sighed as the passages brought back sad memories.

Finally, Dorothy, who was partially of Indian blood, said, "Yes, when our people moved west in those days, they met Indians who'd never seen people who can read and write and have different crafts and professions. The Indians' most valuable possession was the right to hunt and fish. That's how they'd always lived and they were going to die defending that. They couldn't tolerate strangers moving into their territory."

"Yes, but remember many Indians recognized that peace was possible and welcomed settlers," Sally reminded the women. "These letters were written after we won the war, but we still had no constitution. Every state had its own militia and its own currency. Part of the problem was that the British had promised the Indians who supported them that they could keep their land, and that after the war settlers would be restricted from moving into Indian territory. But the British lost the war and couldn't keep their promise. The Indians who were for Washington, like White Eyes, welcomed settlers and wanted peace. Adopting the Constitution and electing Washington as president made a big difference to a lot of Indians."

Jane went inside to put the papers away while the older women took a small lunch meal of vegetable soup and bread. Resting after eating, they remembered and talked about their friends who'd moved west over the past years, how some died, and where their children now lived.

Sally began to doze off in the warmth while Jane stayed in the kitchen with Leven's chest of papers to reread her essay. She had her pen and wrote a few notes to herself. When she finished, she went back to the porch and sipped her mug of cider.

Nancy and Dorothy went into the house and prepared the extra bedrooms. They expected a full house over the next few days. They put on fresh sheets, fluffed up some pillows, and opened the windows to let in some fresh air. When they were finished, they came back to the porch to sit and watch the sun set while Sally still slept in her rocking chair.

Near sundown, they could hear the sounds of horses. They saw three riders, two on horseback leading a mule pulling a wagon and a taller rider on horseback in the rear. The procession was led by a leaping small dog, who raced up the path to the house.

Prince ran up the three steps onto the porch and started barking. All four women stood up out of their chairs, shouting "Welcome!" to the travelers, but the beagle and two cats quickly ran into the house and hid under the living room furniture.

Susan and Daniel jumped off their horses and tied them to a rail near the right side of the porch. They then ran up onto the porch and embraced Nancy, their grandmother. Nancy held onto both and was near tears.

Sally, awakened by the noise of Prince and the other animals, said, "Welcome and rest yourselves. Where's your puppy been that he scared our beagle and two cats just by barking?"

Susan came over to Jane near where Prince now lapped water

from the beagle's bowl. She said, "He's been playing with a bear cub. I guess they had a whiff of that."

"They smelled the cub's mother as well," Jane said. "Maybe you should wash him a bit. There's a barrel of rain water around the back. Clean him up a little before you come in. You and Daniel and Dave might want to wash up a bit too."

Nancy said, "Yes, I'll get you a pot of warm water, some soap and towels. Go around the back and find the barrel. I'll be out shortly."

Dave heard the conversation, but didn't move from the wagon and the mule. He shouted to Sally, "My grandmother has sent some blankets and things. Shall we bring them into the house?"

Sally said, "Just leave them here on the porch and we'll do the rest. Unhitch the mule and get him something to drink. Then go around and wash yourself. We'll have an early dinner. Maybe a celebration! We're anxious to hear what you have to say."

While Dave and Daniel watered and fed the mule and horses, Sally started taking the bundles of hats and blankets into the house. They were heavy, but Susan came back to the house after washing and cleaning up Prince and helped Sally move the blankets into the living room. Sally could see that they showed magnificent colors and geometric patterns. The knitted hats, also brightly colored, were of tightly woven wools.

Sally asked, "What do you think? Are these for old folks that feel the cold?"

Susan laughed and responded, "I wouldn't mind a blanket like that. They are the most beautiful things I've ever seen."

"Yes, Anna Silver makes wonderful things. Well, I'm sure you've been a good and brave girl. Pick one out and take it up to one of the front bedrooms. Try to keep the dog off it."

Susan chose a blanket with a complex design that included numerous triangles in bright yellow and turquoise. She took it up the stairs, followed by Prince, and found a small bedroom where the window was open, causing the lace curtain to move with the light spring breeze. The bed had been freshly made.

When Susan saw the bed, she threw the new blanket on top and placed a pillow on the floor for Prince. She then climbed on top of the bed, pulled up the new blanket, and immediately fell asleep.

After Daniel and Dave tended the mule and the horses, they finished washing up and found some shade under a giant elm near the porch. Both sat down on the ground leaning against different sides of the tree. The sun was setting, but the day remained warm. Within five minutes, both were also asleep.

Dorothy, in the kitchen, warmed some meat pies and placed them in a large pot away from the flames so they would remain warm. She walked out the back door to see if the water barrel had been used, and picked up five wet towels and placed them in the wash barrel. After looking around in the dimming light, she saw the sleeping boys.

She felt great relief at seeing the youngsters and smiled to herself. She went back to the porch and sat down next to Jane. Soon Sally and Nancy were out with a pitcher of cider and some mugs. The four looked at each other until Sally said, "They are weary, but they are here and safe. Let them rest awhile."

Nancy said, "The first time one of those boys moves, he'll feel some discomfort from the roots and twigs on the ground."

"Yes," said Jane. "And with the front door open, they'll also smell the meat pies and likely wake up hungry. What about Susan?"

Nancy said, "She's fast asleep upstairs on a bed. The puppy's asleep on a pillow on the floor beside her. If she's to eat, someone will have to go up and wake her and that will wake up the dog, too."

Sally finally said, "I'll have half a meat pie. Is anyone else hungry?"

Dorothy and Nancy went into the kitchen and brought out a platter of pies, some dishes and some cutlery. The clatter of the dishes wakened the boys who soon were up on the porch and sipping some cider.

Daniel asked, "Where's Susan?"

Sally said, "Sound asleep upstairs, along with the puppy. How about you two? Dorothy will take you up to a bedroom with sheets on the bed. Better than the roots of a tree. You don't look ready to give us a good account of the last week or so."

"I'm not the talker and Dave here didn't come on our journey," Daniel replied. We have to wait for Susan to fill in everything." The two boys ate two meat pies each, but then excused themselves to go upstairs.

An hour later, the house was dark and everyone slept soundly.

CHAPTER 35

TALK ABOUT ADVENTURE

PRINCE WOKE UP as the dawn broke and leaped up onto the bed to lick Susan's face. She reluctantly and slowly woke from a very deep sleep, the first she'd had since they left for the Logan farm almost a week earlier. She felt sharp hunger pains and looked around for something to wear.

She realized her traveling leathers needed to be put away now that she was back in a proper house. She noticed that there was a pile of linens on a chair near the window, but she didn't see her little bag of personal belongings. She remembered she'd left it in the wagon, and someone probably unloaded it downstairs the previous night, but she couldn't remember seeing it.

She looked at the pile of linens but decided they were too fine and probably not meant for her. Instead, she wrapped the new blanket around herself managing to secure it around her waist with her belt. She put on her traveling boots and went down the stairs, followed by Prince.

When she found the kitchen, she saw Dorothy and Jane already having their morning coffee. Dorothy said, "You must be hungry. You fell asleep last night before we could feed you."

Jane looked at Susan and said, "Anna sent a packet for you and one for each of the boys. We unpacked them and left them for you in your rooms. Didn't you see them? They are some nice beaded linens for you to wear while you're in the house. Let us have your travel clothes to hang out and freshen."

"My goodness, I didn't know those nice things were for me. They look so fine."

"Well, darlin', you're a heroine now. You made it back in one piece and we're pleased to have you with us. Let me help you with the new things." With that, Jane and Susan went up the stairs to Susan's bedroom with Susan talking all the way. Dorothy kept Prince downstairs feeding him some coarse grain.

When Susan and Jane came down, the boys were up, wearing fresh new linen shirts, vests and pantaloons, and eating breakfast biscuits. Everyone in the house now was awake and in the kitchen.

Breakfast was long and heavy, with reheated beef and chicken pies, eggs, bacon, porridge, and coffee. Dave finally said, "Mrs. Powell and everyone, I thank you for a wonderful meal, but I really didn't do anything special to deserve this. I just brought Dan and Sue back by the main road."

Sally said, "That's more than enough to earn a breakfast. We hope you'll all stay here until the party from Winchester arrives in the next few days. Then you'll have real news for your folks. First, tell us about your journey to Logan's and the Black Eagle. We're anxious to hear all of it."

Daniel began slowly, relating the relatively uneventful journey to Logan's farm. Susan talked about the trees and the flowers, how Prince sniffed everything along the way, and how hot it was when they arrived. Then they began the full story, on meeting Beth, exchanging rifles with the Logan boys, and getting Henry Logan's instructions on how to get through the wood.

Sally asked, "So Beth went with you to the Black Eagle through the woods, while John stayed with Burr?"

Susan replied, "Yes, she was anxious to talk to her Uncle Billy. Her Dad left her at Logan's and she shared a room with Hannah and Amy, but when we got there, she was anxious to come with us. She actually wanted to go through the woods. There was talk about a visiting bear and bear cub, and we had a bag of honey biscuits with us."

Then both Susan and Daniel told about how they got through the woods, about crossing the creeks following a black bear and her cub, and about fishing in the creek. Susan said, "The mother bear really frightened Prince, but I left a honey biscuit for the bear cub and he grabbed it quickly. We didn't see them after that, not till we got to the Black Eagle."

Susan added, "Bobby guided the mule, King George, and got himself cold and wet. Beth gave him her jacket."

Daniel continued, "And she left biscuits for the bear cub when we got to the clearing near the second creek. When we got to the place, Beth was attacked from behind by two men coming out of the woods. The mother bear came out of the woods and saved her, swatting that varmint hard over the head. Both of them ran away."

Susan added, "Yes. Bobby managed to get a shot off but it went way up in the air. Beth was lucky the bear followed us."

The four women looked at each other, "That's so hard to believe. So everyone is unhurt? Beth and Bobby?"

Dave said, "Yes, when everyone got to my grandparents at the Black Eagle, we had a magician with us. Marcus thought the bear might have been his, one who ran away the previous year. He put on a show for us and the neighbors and the mother and cub showed up. The mother bear did a dance on top of a platform attached to a ladder. Beth and Susan both helped with the performance."

Sally sat down and exclaimed, "What a story! When did you see Burr? Or did you? What of Burr and John?

Dave continued, "Mr. Burr Powell and John arrived at the Black

Eagle before Marcus put on his show. They were in the tavern when it began, but came back to see us after it was over. Mr. Burr talked to my grandfather, who called out to our local militia to go to Winchester to help out Billy. The Powells took a buggy by the main road to the Golden Sparrow in Winchester. Beth and Bobby stayed with my grandfather and went through the woods to Winchester with our militia. Dan, Sue and I came here with my grandmother's packages. The Black Eagle seemed really crowded with lots of people from far away. That's all we know about what's happening."

"Well, you've told a great story," Dorothy said. "Let's wait together to see how this ends. What would you like to do today? Rest or do a little work around the yard?"

Susan said, "It's warm. Can we go fishing this afternoon? Maybe we can catch something for dinner."

Jane agreed. "Let me come with you. We'll take the horses down to the creek. Some fish will be jumping, I'm sure."

"That's a good idea. Rest up and bring us dinner," Nancy said. "We'll do some baking while we wait for you. Maybe we'll read you some historical stuff about Mr. Leven, too."

They changed out of their linen clothes and into some heavier coarse things suitable for a fishing afternoon. These were old clothes left behind by some of the Powell children in the various bedrooms. Jane took the buggy, which included a bucket of worms for bait and a few fishing rods.

When they left, Sally, Nancy and Dorothy sat on the porch. Sally asked, "What do you make of that story? Beth, my granddaughter, friends with wild bears?"

Dorothy replied, "Sounds more like she's made friends with Bobby. I think they are both a little young for anything to be concerned about, but a trip through the wild woods will be something for both to remember."

CHAPTER 36
BACK FROM WINCHESTER

A T MIDDAY, WHILE sitting in her rocking chair on the porch three days later, Sally heard the loud sounds of horses and could see quite a large party coming up the path. Everyone inside the house heard the noise. They came out onto the porch and started shouting "Welcome!" and "They're here!"

Billy and George on horseback were the first to arrive, followed by Burr and John in a buggy, followed by Beth and Bobby on horseback. Two additional riders unfamiliar to Sally came up behind them.

Dave, Daniel and Susan came down off the porch to help with the horses and buggy while Beth and Bobby ran up onto the porch to embrace their grandmothers. John helped his father out of the buggy and Billy handed Burr his cane. Billy then leaped up onto the porch to tell his mother, "All is well. Hardly a shot was fired and the politicians won the day." He embraced Sally and hugged her.

Sally stood almost in tears, with Beth and Jane standing next to her. Soon John and Burr arrived and also embraced Sally.

From the porch, Burr announced, "There is good news, but the details can wait. We've brought a ham and some deer meat with us for a fine celebration. Let's cook out this afternoon. The travelers will do all the work."

Sally sat down again, but Nancy and Dorothy spoke to Burr and Billy, "Sirs, you will first wash up, remove your travel clothes, and find your bedrooms inside. You are still Powells and today is no different than any other day. We'll give you aprons when it's time to prepare the food."

Jane stood back from all of the greetings, pleased to see everyone well, but staring at George Morgan White Eyes. In five years, he'd changed much more than his years. Still very tall, his shoulders now were broad and his prominent nose and high cheekbones reminded her of someone else, but she couldn't place exactly whom.

George also stayed back with the two riders who were part of his tribe and children of revolutionary war veterans who'd settled in Ohio. He looked at Jane and Sally and thought, "We are all older than before. How much of my father do they remember?"

When the greetings had died down and Billy and Burr moved back to the wash barrel, George approached the porch. He slowly came up the stairs and said to Sally, "Greetings, Mrs. Powell. I understand that Mr. Leven has left this world. Perhaps he's looking down on us with my father, White Eyes." When he said this, he bowed to Jane. "I hope you are well. You look fine to me, finer than I can remember. These few years have been kind to you. I hope we can take some time to talk. I have much to tell about Billy and Ohio."

Jane said nothing, but Sally stood up, moved toward George and hugged him. She said, "What a relief to see you. We feared you were dead or worse. Yes, Leven left us some weeks ago, but he remembered your father and Washington as the best people he'd known in this life. You'll always be welcome here, George."

George replied, "Perhaps I should pitch a tent in the back; you have quite a full house now."

Sally said, "No, you and your friends are our guests. Nancy will sort out the bedrooms. We raised ten children here, you remember, and you're all welcome. You and your friends can go back to the wash barrel and make yourselves comfortable. We have clothes upstairs for you to change to, and we should all rest a bit before we eat."

Jane turned, saying nothing, and went into the house where she found Beth and Susan in the kitchen. She said, "Why don't you go up and change, Beth? I'll bring up a washbowl, some warm water, soap and a towel. You can share the room with Susan for now."

Beth couldn't restrain herself. "Oh, Aunt Jane, I don't want to stay here in Middleburg. I want to go to Ohio. Can you talk to Father?"

Jane said, "We all need to do a lot of thinking and talking, and we still don't know what's up with Billy. We'll talk later today after I understand things a little better."

George stood at the entrance to the kitchen and heard the conversation. He stood aside as the girls went up the stairs and said to Jane:

"Can we take a walk together? I remember your little creek behind the house where we once fished together. We could take some wine and sit under the trees awhile."

Jane sputtered, "I haven't seen you in five years or heard from you in all that time. I'd love to hear what you have to say." She quickly turned away, carrying a pitcher of clean water, soap, and a towel and ran up the stairs to Susan's room where Beth and Susan were waiting.

Susan had placed all the clothes she had on the bed for Beth to see. When Jane entered, Beth said, "Oh, Aunt Jane, talk to George about Ohio. There must be a way for me to go. I think John is not so happy to try things out west, but George and he had some talks in the woods. Father was pleased with what they were saying, but I don't know the details."

"Well, maybe I'll find out in the next few hours. Here's some clean water and soap. Get ready for a nice meal. We all have a lot to be thankful for."

Jane went to her room and sat on her bed for a few minutes. She didn't know what to do. Change her clothes? Be angry? About what?

She went down to the kitchen and found her essay about Leven. She thought about disappearing somewhere with a pen and paper, but that didn't seem practical now. Where could she go now? All the upstairs rooms were taken. She knew she had to face facts. Everyone around her, those who cared about her, planned to make decisions for her. She knew she had to make her own decisions now. She left the essay and went out onto the porch where George was talking to her mother.

Jane said, "Mother, rest now. Burr's announced that the visitors will prepare the food. See that Nancy and Dorothy don't do too much either. George and I will take a walk down the back toward the creek."

Sally smiled. "Wonderful to have you back, George, and us all together again. Take your time. You have much to talk about." Sally reclined in the rocking chair, and soon both Nancy and Dorothy joined her with a pitcher of cider.

George motioned to one of his men, who came up to the porch carrying a bottle of wine. The man said to Sally, "Mrs. Powell, I am Ed Walker. My father served under Washington at Valley Forge, as did Mr. Leven. I'm here to visit some cousins in Alexandria. May I join you all for a glass of wine?" Burr came out of the house and pulled up a chair.

George winked at Sally. "They've made arrangements for him, I think." With that, he turned toward Jane, took her arm and helped her down the porch steps. They walked slowly toward the creek, deep in conversation.

CHAPTER 37

CELEBRATION

GEORGE AND JANE sat beneath an old oak tree, sipping wine from a large red jug he'd carried on his back on the way from the house. They'd been talking about relatively mundane things, including Sally's health, how the flour mill was doing, and the progress of Leven's turnpike that was planned to stretch from Alexandria to Winchester.

When they both were relaxed, George said, "I know Billy spoke with Cuthbert about me the last time he came back. Do you know anything about how I came to Ohio and the rest?" George looked at Jane and saw her intelligent eyes and strong posture. He knew she wouldn't lie to him.

Jane replied, "What he told me he said was secondhand. That you'd been tracked by Jefferson's agents who aimed to kill you; how your Indian cousins protected you; that you took an Indian wife who died in childbirth but left you with a son. Is your boy well? How old is he now? Who cares for him?"

George replied, "You have the general sense, but you can't really appreciate what's happened unless you come and see Ohio. It's a vast country with great rivers and miles of flat farmland. Not like Virginia or New Jersey at all. My boy, who I named George

Washington White Eyes, is now a little past two years old. He is tall
and bright and needs a mother. I take that back. He's being cared
for by his mother's parents now. He doesn't simply need someone
who'll care for him; he needs you. He and I both need your warmth,
your strength, your judgment, your ability to decide things and be
a leader."

Jane was surprised at George's directness, but that reminded
her that he'd always been direct and decisive. She remembered
that he'd been an ardent follower of Aaron Burr, even after the
Hamilton assassination. George had swallowed all of the philosophy
associated with that. He believed in building a new country that
really had equality, where everyone who worked had the vote,
including women. He was a college graduate and spoke in a refined
way, but his beliefs were true to the core.

Jane said, "Are you asking me to come with you, or are you asking
me to become your wife? I have some obligations here, and we need
to agree on what you are proposing before we go any further."

George replied, "I have always wanted to ask you to be my wife.
I would have raised the matter with Leven five years ago, but that
was no journey for a woman. I barely survived myself. Now I have
spoken with Billy and Burr and your mother. I believe they will all
support our marriage. So will Cuthbert. I'm now asking you: will
you take me as your husband?"

Jane started weeping. She hated being the center of attention
and this, she knew, would upstage everything that Billy and Burr
had planned.

George waited and offered her a handkerchief, but she kept
sobbing.

He said, "Is that how terrible the thought of marriage is? Is it
me? My little boy? Ohio? You will be my treasured wife, the wife
of a member of the Ohio Congress, and possibly soon of the U. S.
Congress. You will not have a sumptuous house, but you will have a

house and be comfortable. You can bring Beth and any other of your nieces and nephews, if you like. I know that Beth will be happy to come. But Ohio is a wild place. There is more danger from attacks from Indians and bandits. In fact, we still have the threat of wars with Tecumseh's federation, and I don't know how we'll be if we have another war with the British. You won't be going to a safe, secure place."

Jane finally spoke, "We've both lived through wars before. That doesn't frighten me. I know my country and what I believe. But I am not the young girl I once was. I'm still fit and able, and can be a help to a member of Congress. Mainly, I'm a teacher. I helped raise my brothers and you know them well. I think I could be a good mother for your little boy. George, even though there is trouble in the world, this time I want a real marriage. I want a proper wedding for all friends and family to see us joined together."

George looked at Jane and smiled. "None of us conspirators thought of that. I promise you will have your wedding, in any place you want it, with whomever you want to invite. It will be like Leven were here watching. I will be proud to stand up next to you."

Jane, finally smiling, said, "Well, we have things to think about and prepare. I know Beth would love to come to Ohio. What of John?"

George replied, "I'm ahead of you there. I have written to the dean at the College of New Jersey, and informed them that two new students, John Powell and Robert Potter of Virginia will be arriving for the fall semester. Their fees will be paid from my trust, which the U. S. Congress established for my education when my parents were killed. Burr is delighted with the idea that his son will receive a formal education. I hope Bobby's parents will allow it. He's a very brave boy. He saved Beth's life in the Winchester woods."

"I suppose Cuthbert will take them up to New Jersey?" Jane

wondered. "You have thought out a lot of things. I hope the plans work as intended."

George looked at Jane. "I'm so pleased you waited for me. Now this afternoon can be a real celebration."

George helped Jane up as they heard footsteps approaching. Bobby, Beth, Susan, Daniel and John, dressed for fishing and pulling a small wagon of gear, had come to the creek.

Beth exclaimed, "There you are! Everyone is looking for you. The cooking has begun. We thought if we catch a few fish, we can fry them up quickly, too. We're supposed to tell you to speak to my father, who's sitting on a tree stump and ordering everyone else around. Uncle Billy's lying down upstairs on his bed."

Jane smiled. "Yes, your dad is used to that; so is your uncle. We'll see what we can do to help."

When they got back to the house, George asked to speak to Sally while Jane entered to kitchen to see what she could do. Nancy and Dorothy were cutting vegetables, making potato salad, and watching over the baking. Dorothy looked at Jane, smiling, and asked, "Do you have something to tell your mother?"

"No, but George is talking to her now. I suppose he'll also have something to say to Billy and Burr as well. What would you say to another Powell wedding?"

The two women dropped what they were doing and both embraced Jane. Nancy said, "For the wedding, you'll have something sweet, to sweeten the future. God bless you; it's been a long time coming."

Dorothy said, "And we'll want some poetry, to set the right mood. The new Methodist minister, people say, was once an actor in Philadelphia. Mrs. Powell always insisted on Episcopal weddings. We'll be ready, whatever you say. You've been a fine daughter to Ms. Sally and you deserve a handsome fellow like George; he'll make a good husband."

Two hours later, the household assembled for an afternoon

feast and Burr addressed the crowd, now even larger, as some neighbors had come over, bringing more food. He said, "Thank you all for coming. We welcome everyone to our celebration of the safe return of our brother Billy and of George Morgan White Eyes. Tomorrow, we go to Alexandria to complete the legal issues facing Billy's ownership of land in Ohio. The matters are only a formality and should be done without difficulty. We will return quickly as George has asked for the hand of our sister Jane in marriage. We are delighted and invite all to a proper wedding, to be held here at the Powell home in two weeks. George and Jane will then leave for Ohio."

Two weeks later, George and Jane were married in a formal Episcopal ceremony, with contributions by the local Methodist minister and a speech by the leading Quaker preacher of the county. All of the wedding orations wished the bride and groom a happy future and mentioned that they were venturing to a new state that had been surveyed by George Washington. All of them also mentioned Leven and the importance of his building the road that now went all the way from Alexandria to Winchester. In attendance were more than five hundred people, including virtually all of the Powells, their aunts, uncles and cousins, as well as friends from Loudoun County, Leesburg and Alexandria.

On the journey to Ohio, George and Jane were joined by two of Jane's nieces. Beth and Amy Powell, Cuthbert's fourteen-year old daughter, were close in age and looked like sisters. Both were energetic and blond and loved the outdoors. Jane left her essay in the box of Leven's papers which she asked Burr to take.

EPILOGUE
LETTER FROM JANE, 1816

THE POST BETWEEN Middleburg and southern Ohio came infrequently. Cuthbert and Burr received letters from Jane about twice a year. She often tried to get Billy to add something, but generally she did all the writing.

From Cuthbert's letters, Jane learned of her mother's death in 1812, and the deaths of both Nancy and Dorothy the following year. With that news, Jane felt a complete chapter of her life had ended. She'd never written to her mother to tell her she lost her first baby in 1811, thinking not to add to the woes of her old mother. She also never mentioned that warfare seemed to be simmering among the tribes. By 1812, the whole country was at war again with the British.

Jane and little George immediately took to each other, and she surprised herself by becoming a doting mother. He was a very happy three-year old and not ready for school. Jane occupied him with games and stories and began to teach him a little reading.

Jane had intended to start a school in her first year, but felt poorly most of that time. Food seemed not to agree with her, nor did carrying a baby. George was a kind and caring husband, and Beth and Amy were a great help, especially when the baby was due.

But the loss of the little boy in childbirth left Jane weakened and saddened. She did very little until becoming very bored and, after two months, she put her energy into starting a small school. Little George would soon be four and ready to learn.

Marcus established an outdoor circus with permanent tents and added a few jugglers and singers to his entertainment. Beth often went over to help him with the bear show and made some posters to help drum up business. She also spent time with the bears and was amazed at how large Blackbeard had grown that first year. Marcus tried to train him, but feared he would soon run away to the woods along the river.

Amy had grown to be a very pretty girl, but was very shy about meeting the local boys. They were rough and wild compared to the boys in Alexandria, and a long procession formed every Saturday of boys asking her to picnics, fishing, dances, the circus, or whatever she wanted. Her new Uncle George insisted on meeting every boy she went with, and often refused to let her go.

Beth had developed admirers, too, but she kept up a correspondence with Bobby, hoping he'd come to Ohio when he finished his education in New Jersey. In 1812, Bobby joined the U. S. Army and was deployed to Maryland for the war against the British. Correspondence with him became very sparse.

War came with a vengeance to the western territories in 1812, but most of the fighting took place in the north. The tribes around Cincinnati opposed the British and were willing to fight for the new country. Jack Walsh quickly enlisted in William Henry Harrison's army that chased the British and their Indian allies into Ontario, Canada. There the Shawnee chief Tecumseh died and his confederacy of tribes died with him. Without Tecumseh, most of the Indian braves fighting the Americans went back to their villages.

After the war ended in 1814, John Powell came to Ohio as an

apprentice and administrator for a ship building firm that specialized in steamships for navigation on the Ohio River. He was well spoken and very interested in science and industry. He took a small room in the town near the river and looked forward to the arrival of Bobby the following year. Classmates in New Jersey, they'd talked about doing something together when they got settled.

When Bobby arrived in 1815, he was twenty-one and Beth was eighteen. Though they'd corresponded to some extent before the war broke out, they were no longer the young teenagers who'd made their way through the woods. Encouraged by John, Beth's brother, Bobby began his courtship of Beth by asking permission from George and Jane. George insisted that he establish himself first, and suggested he speak with Jack Walsh.

Though he'd once shot him in the leg, Bobby struck up a friendship with Jack, as now they both were veterans of the same war. By 1815, Walsh had a stake in Ohio. He had a business, was the father of three and his wife had become good friends with Jane, wife of the local representative to the state legislature.

Jack began a business in Cincinnati selling leather goods and Indian crafts as he knew where to get fine woolens and blankets and ladies' hats. Bobby knew those materials very well, as many were made by his relatives. Jack offered Bobby a stake in the business if he would see to the books and advertising, since Bobby had studied law and accounting in New Jersey. Bobby accepted the position, and three weeks later he and Beth married.

Bobby and Jack agreed that after a year, Bobby would buy into the business and become a partner. As a wedding present, Beth's Uncle Billy agreed to give Bobby the necessary cash. Billy had become quite well off from collecting rent from farmers who'd settled on his properties along the Ohio. Towns and farms had sprung up in all directions around Cincinnati.

In late 1816, Jane sent the following letter to Cuthbert, with an enclosure for Burr:

We are enjoying the arrival of peace, with good news to tell. In February, I was able to bring a lovely little girl into the world. We have named her Sarah and call her Sally, and she is the most important person in the lives of both my Georges.

Beth gave birth to a fine-looking little boy just before the new year. She has named him Leven after her grandfather, but if the baby were a she, Beth would have insisted on Louise for the bear who saved her life in the woods. How strange for me, Beth's aunt, to have a first child the same time she has hers. The babies will be like brother and sister.

Amy, lovely as ever, still hasn't decided from among the forty or so boys who express an interest in her. She prefers to teach at the little school and writes long essays for herself which she never shows anyone. I'm afraid being present at the birthing of my poor firstborn has frightened her. She hasn't gotten over seeing the pain, mess and aftermath.

John has shown an interest in a Lenape girl, granddaughter to Red Feather, George's first cousin. Red Feather, you may remember, came to Winchester and left early, taking Jack Walsh with him back to Ohio. Sadly, Red Feather was killed in a skirmish against the British somewhere up north.

George seems to approve of the possible marriage of John Powell to Helen Red Feather. If the marriage happens, it will be soon. Do you think Burr will like this idea?

The state capital is once again to be moved, this time to Columbus which is closer to the middle of the state and a distance from where we live. George is a loyal representative of the people who live near us, and has served in the state legislature for eight years now. He is thinking of running for the U. S. Congress from our district. If that should happen, we might consider buying a house for our small family in Alexandria. Perhaps we'll bring Amy back with us. She might be happier with you at home.

I enclose a short enclosure for Burr, who has the chest with Father's papers and the beginnings of my essay. Please share this letter and the enclosure with all the family.

Enclosure for Burr:

Burr, you have my essay taken from Father's papers. Perhaps you have finished it yourself by now. I would do the whole thing over. I'm now an older and wiser person, and have a different attitude toward memorials now. I've seen a lot of death and suffering over the last few years, and that is part of life as we know it.

First, Father needs no special memorial and he wouldn't have liked one. His presence speaks through his accomplishments. These are his family, you and yours included, Middleburg (which could have been called Powell Town, but Father refused that), and the turnpike from Alexandria to Winchester which, as a member of the U. S. Congress, Father arranged to be built.

Beyond that, Father is survived by his voting record. He was the only Virginian to back Adams over Jefferson in the 1796 Electoral College. In 1800, he supported Jefferson as President, but that was because Jefferson had agreed to a deal with Aaron Burr. Father disliked Jefferson as devious and unreliable. He thought Jefferson loved the French, aristocracy, slavery and had contempt for our Constitution. I remember Father considered Burr to be vastly superior to Jefferson. I think he described Burr as having a mind "fearless of the bold."

My George, as you know, loves Aaron Burr, and today I live in Burr country. We have no class of landed planters and slave holders, and the towns are being built from the ground up by new arrivals from many places. Aaron Burr favors a vote for everyone who works, and Jefferson feared that. I think, from where I sit, the future will be written by people who follow Burr's beliefs.

Cuthbert, I believe now that everyone has a memorial and it's inscribed in the minds of the children, students and workers that live with and near us. The ideas we share are sent down to the next generation. For Father, those ideas started with Washington, as did his will to move west. I think we here in Ohio are just the latest example of people operating willingly in Washington's shadow. There will be many more after us.

Author's Note and Acknowledgements

WASHINGTON'S SHADOW is the product of some two years' research when I served as a volunteer in the history section of the Jamestown Yorktown Foundation. At the time, preparations were being made for the building of the American Revolution Museum at Yorktown, an institution which is now open. I worked for Ed Ayres, historian, who collected materials about persons alive during the revolution who he thought would be of interest to future museum visitors.

For a year or so, I went through various documents and previous reports, and came up with a list of people who were of interest to me. I can't say why they interested me, but I found Leven Powell's correspondence fundamentally funny. In a way he was like me. He found himself in unique historical circumstances, surrounded by truly great and historic people, but he remained ordinary. His goals were prosaic and easy to see. He knew where he wanted to go, tried very hard to get there, and was honest to a fault.

Washington's Shadow is a novel. All of the characters are fictional, though the historical events described and Leven's correspondence are factual and verifiable. Wherever possible, the letters of Leven included in this book are taken directly from the original sources. Leven did serve in the electoral college of 1796 and in the U. S. Congress. He was responsible for the building of Middleburg, Virginia and the highway, now known as Route 50, from Alexandria to Winchester.

Source material came from the Jamestown Yorktown Foundation and from the Manuscripts Department of the Earl Gregg Swem Library, The College of William and Mary. The William and Mary collection includes the correspondence of Leven Powell from 1774 through 1806, a collection of ninety-three items, most documents written by Leven, others to him.

In addition, I found some materials about Leven in the Biographical Directory of the U. S. Congress, in J. H. Gwatney's *Historical Register of Virginians in the Revolution* (The Dietz Press, Richmond, 1938), and Louis A. Burgess, ed., *Virginia Soldiers of 1776* (Richmond Press, Inc, 1929). The annual publication of the John P. Branch Historical Papers of Randolph-Macon College (Everett Waddey Company) devoted its issue to Leven Powell in 1905.

Information about the origins of Middleburg came from the National Register of Historic Places (continuation sheet, Section 8, page 6). An address by James D. Evans at the unveiling of a mural tablet to the memory of Leven and his wife in the Episcopal Church in Middleburg on the occasion of the 200th anniversary of their births was published in *The William and Mary Quarterly*, Vol. 19, No. 2, April 1939.

Information about the revolution and the immediate post-revolutionary period was taken from general and popular sources. For Aaron Burr, I consulted Gore Vidal's novel, *Burr* (1973) and Nancy Isenberg, *Fallen Founder, The life of Aaron Burr* (2008). For background and information on early elections and show trials, I consulted William H. Rehnquist, *Grand Inquests* (1992) and Jensen and Becker, *The Documentary History of the First Federal Elections, 1788-1790* (1976).

For other historic figures of the period, I made use of Marty D. Matthews, *Forgotten Founder, The Life and Times of Charles Pinckney* (2004), Ron Chernow, *Alexander Hamilton* (2004) and *Washington* (2010), and Marvin Kitman, *George Washington's Expense Account* (1970).

Finally, I would like to thank those whose help was essential for the publication of this book. My writers critique group, part of the Chesapeake Bay Writers Association, provided early comments and suggestions. Gatekeeper Press provided editing, design and formatting services. For Gatekeeper Press, Kelly Branchal provided detailed, thoughtful, and supportive editing; Joshua Kaplan skillfully designed the cover, patiently incorporating some of my suggestions; and Sarah Spencer provided overall management of the publication process.

Last, but not least, my oncologist and surgeons at the Medical Center of Virginia (VCU) in Richmond gave me courage while over the past year I received treatment for lymphoma. The doctors and nurses filled me with hope and confidence, giving me the energy to complete this book. I never thought about being sick when I worked on *Washington's Shadow*.